I0675888

Lies To Live By

Stories

by

Fred Misurella

Bordighera

Library of Congress Cataloguing-in-Publication Data

Misurella, Fred, 1940–
    Lies to live by : stories / by Fred Misurella.
        p. cm. -- (VIA folios ; 38)
        ISBN 1-884419-72-0
        1. Italian Americans--Social life and customs--Fiction. I. Title.
II. Series.

PS3563.I7353L54 2005
813′.54--dc22

2005055332

*The characters and events in these stories are fictitious.
Any similiarity to real persons, living or dead, is
coincidental and not intended by the author.*

© 2005 Fred Misurella.

All rights reserved. Parts of this book may be reprinted only by
written permission from the author, and may not be reproduced
for publication in book, magazine, or electronic media of any kind,
except in quotations for purposes of literary reviews by critics.

Printed in the United States.

Published by
BORDIGHERA PRESS
Languages and Linguistics
Florida Atlantic University
Boca Raton, FL 33431

VIA FOLIOS 38
ISBN 1-884419-72-0

For Kim

Acknowledgements

In slightly different form, "Parenting" and "Relations" have appeared in *The Kansas Quarterly*; "Body Lessons" and "A Man of His Time" in *VIA* (*Voices in Italian Americana*); "Flames" (in French as "Flammes") in *L'Atelier du Roman*; and "Macho Maudit" in *Kestrel*. "Short Time" appeared as a *VIA* FOLIO, published by Bordighera, and was supported by a Creative Writing Fellowship from the Commonwealth of Pennsylvania Council on the Arts. Thanks to the Kansas State Arts Council and East Stroudsburg University for their support. Finally, thanks to Alex Misurella for the use of his drawing, "Starry Night," and to Gene Misurella for his advice on the cover design.

Without realizing it, the individual composes
his life according to the laws of beauty
even in times of greatest distress.

— Milan Kundera

CONTENTS

I. MONEY, LOVE, ART

"Parenting" • 11

"Relations" • 28

"Body Lessons" • 44

"Flames" • 60

"A Man of His Time" • 74

II. AMERICA

"Macho Maudit" • 89

"The Dragon Lady and the Soldier" • 111

"Short Time" • 127

MONEY, LOVE, ART

PARENTING

*H*is wife, Elaine, had been a doctor, a general practitioner in this little Pennsylvania town. In her own home she was as neurotic about escaping fluids and structural weaknesses of the body as Bevacqua could be about the changing seasons. Pain, his, their child's, or her own, threw her into a state of panic. Urine that did not have the right color, feces a little too loose or a little too formed were cause for laboratory investigation. And everything sharp, loose, or high about the house needed to be covered or tied down.

Elaine had cared too much, he thought; she had been a saint who made house calls after midnight, even in winter, sat for hours in vigils with patients until they died or recovered. Once she told him that she regarded her presence as the only certain way of warding off the final breath. And yet her body erupted on its own — just fifteen years before this autumn — a cancer that spread like fire, destroying the landscape of her flesh until she was left a skeleton, tied, cathetered, skin drawn tight across her skull and breathless chest, her eyes pleading with him for release, at the same time something deeper seemed to cling to life. Finally, her breath whispering, her chest heaving, he felt a flutter of her hand, and, as if her body were a tree battling a violent storm, the wind stopped and she went still.

He was not sickly or depressed, he said. He increased his running from five to fifteen miles a day, cut down on meats, salts, and sugars, yet with each passing autumn, as if October clouds carried a special message for him, he felt a greater heaviness in his limbs, a narrower passage of air from mouth and nose to heart and lungs, and a less certain pulse of blood beating through his limbs as it, like Elaine, carried relief and health to the outer provinces and islands of his body.

"I just don't have it anymore," he had said this year, after his usual end of September marathon meet. "I think I'm going to have to cut out these races."

An insurance broker, a former college football player, he was more than a weekend athlete, and his daughter, Carla, had listened to his announcement with a smile. Standing like a newly dissected specimen before the mirror, he had examined himself and his issue. Amazed at the bald head, the wrinkles, the slight paunch (despite hours and hours of sit ups), the closer alignment of skin to bone around the jaw and eyes, he could not escape the fact that he was changing, becoming less robust before Carla's eyes. At twenty-five he had thought of himself as thirty-five. At fifty he could think of himself as barely approaching forty.

"You look great, Daddy. Don't worry about it."

He turned from the mirror and looked at her, sprawling spider-like on the living room sofa, with the light from the gloomy day outside silvering her hair. She studied anthropology. She was home for the weekend because she had spent the summer in New York and, she said, missed him. She wore jeans and a sweater, and was reading Claude Levi-Strauss (in French) while balancing a Swedish clog, counterweight to all that serious thought, on the tip of her rather lengthy toes.

"You can say that, honey. But at your age you have a rather vague idea of what's ahead in life."

Carla smiled. "I know what I see in front of me, Daddy."

He flexed his biceps and studied some rough-textured spots on his forearm. "I'll have to stay in the sun less next summer. And I think you should too. Especially since you've got your mother's sensitive skin."

Carla nodded, grinning and raising her pale forearm. She had come home to tell him something as well as to visit, and he started to think about what she had said the night before. "It's a boy, a lover," she had announced, breathlessly, as if it were a sacred subject.

Thinking of Elaine and knowing she would want him to accept the news, he had simply nodded, despite the thumping in his chest, and said, "Yes," before adding, "it's only natural."

They had been sitting at dinner, two-thirds of a threesome after all these years, and like a pair of old lovers, they smiled and shrugged together, accepting the inevitable. Bevacqua remembered a similar conversation with his widowed father after becoming engaged to Elaine, and like a man working through a time warp, he glanced at the calendar on the kitchen wall and tried to fix a date. September; he had spoken to his father sometime in the spring. He took a forkful of spaghetti, carbohydrates for the race tomorrow, and bit into it.

"We don't want to get married," Carla said. "But we do want to spend our time together."

He nodded, sucking on the pasta as if it were a particularly tasty marrowbone. "I imagine so," he managed to let out. "That's the way things go nowadays."

More than a year later, on the road across New Jersey to the hospital and her lover, he would remember that moment vividly, recalling precisely how her jaw muscles had twitched, her neck stiffened, and her fingers went to her abdomen as if, impossible he knew, the kick of a future event were already beneath her hand. He had looked to the third chair as if Elaine were sitting there, and laid his fork and spoon down carefully. Tomato clinged to the fork, and pieces of mushroom that looked like bits of flesh.

"His name?"

"Mark."

He looked at his napkin and wanted to bite it.

"Mark what, honey?"

"Greenberg. He's a graduate student in anthropology. I met him in one of my classes."

"Swell."

Time warped for Bevacqua again. Elaine had been Jewish. His father, despite old country views, had taken the news of it as if it were normal. Yet anachronistically, Bevacqua pictured other ire-arousing images: boots, jeans, long hair, and a beard. He remembered male students, their fists raised above their heads, chanting anti-American slogans in the 1960s. "No dope," he said, thinking of his father. "I mean I hope he doesn't use or smoke any. I'm sure he's very intelligent."

Carla had shaken her head. "He's a health-nut, Daddy. He runs around Central Park, and up and down Riverside Drive every day. He doesn't even drink beer."

He pictured a muscular athlete like himself, or at least one of those lean, wiry tennis-playing types with well-built calves and thighs. Instead, Mark was slight, short, stubborn. He showed an angry intelligence in his eyes that dared the world to test him. When they met, Bevacqua was sure that his daughter's skinny lover (bearded, as Bevacqua had feared, but closely cropped, without the sloppiness of a protester) could circle Central Park in a taxi only and that his concern for health would be limited to safe passage home through a moderately threatening street crowd.

"Hello. I'm John Bevacqua."

"Mark Greenberg, Mr. Bevacqua. Hello."

"You're in anthropology."

"Theoretical."

"Theoretical anthropology?"

"Yes." Mark smirked. "That means I read a lot and think about social structures that mess up human lives."

But Carla loved him and, despite the edge that cut into their conversations, Bevacqua tried to love him too. When, six months later, she again came home for a weekend, blooming instead of spider-like, he perceived at once the news that she was carrying. Picturing Elaine, he shouted "*Oh, no!*" the moment Carla walked through the front door.

"What? Daddy, please! What's the matter?"

Someone seemed to walk beside him as he leaned against the wall and stared at his daughter as if she were far away.

"You're pregnant! This is not supposed to happen. Your mother and I told you that for years. This weasel —"

Carla chortled. Her curly hair brushed against his chin as she moved next to him, and he remembered with disdainful bitterness that that same blonde hair towered above the father-to-be with the same distance as his did above hers.

"Daddy, you're so sensitive. How did you know?"

He pushed her to arms' length and looked at her again. "My god, you know you're diabetic. You have to be careful about these things."

Carla smiled, inwardly. She blushed as never before, with none of the pain or angst that Elaine would have shown. "I have been careful," she said. "Daddy, this is planned."

She threw off her coat as if it were a veil and drew Bevacqua's hand to her abdomen. It was slightly rounded, its protuberance on her slim frame like a hillock on a flat horizon. But it was warm, warmer that the rest of her, as if a fire burned within and as if, should it not be released, it would consume the life surrounding it.

"You want to be a doctor," Bevacqua said. "You haven't even completed your B.A."

Carla shook her head, frowning. "First things first, Daddy. I'm healthy now. I want to be a woman. Mark will put me through medical school later on."

"An anthropologist? Since when are they getting jobs?"

"Mark's very good at his work, Daddy."

"He reads. So does everyone else. There's such a thing as demand."

Carla frowned. "I'm sure he'll find something. He has a part time teaching post already."

Bevacqua grunted and sat on a living room chair. He would remember it as the hardest single moment of his life since Elaine had died. Two powerful hands gripped his shoulders. A head seemed to brush against his cheek and press him back. He looked out the window to a gray March twilight and thought, involuntarily, that it had to be fall.

"When is it due?" he asked, finally.

"September. Maybe October. At this point the doctor isn't perfectly sure."

"Does he know about the diabetes? He's going to have to watch this very carefully."

Carla nodded, smiling. She was almost bovine, completely unlike her mother, who had been sharp, fierce, until the cancer burned her independent spirit from her. It was only when Carla had proven to be diabetic that she had lost that strength — and never completely.

"He wants you to go through with it?" Bevacqua asked. "Mark — even with the complications?"

She nodded. "Daddy, things have improved. I won't be the only diabetic woman delivering a child. They're even having full-term childbirths now."

"Who's the doctor? Is he good?"

Carla nodded. "Mark's uncle recommended him. He's one of the best in the Northeast. Mark's going to assist at the birth. If you want to, you can too."

Bevacqua sighed, frowning. He had missed Carla's entrance into the world because he had been away on business. Feeling responsible, he remembered the thousands of needles his wife had injected into Carla's skinny, infant arms, the hundreds of visits to her pediatrician, and the scores of times when she grew faint, lost control of her tongue, or forgot, like an amnesiac, where she was going or who she was. The hands seemed to press more heavily on his shoulders now, but he did not know what to ask. Finally, he said, "The birth. You're sure it will be natural?" The hands tightened; he tried to remember the complications surrounding the childbirths of diabetic women.

"I hope so," Carla said. She stepped back, less certain for the moment. "Unless the... Unless my baby gets too big.

Then we'll deliver by Caesarean."

Bevacqua moaned. The mere thought of more metal invading her body made him sick.

"It should never have happened," he shouted, closing his eyes.

He felt Carla's arms around him as she kneeled beside his chair. His head sank into his hands. Something loosened from his shoulder as he looked up. With a burst of cool March wind, it rushed through the still open living room door and slammed it shut.

She became one of those beautiful russet pears that he always associated with October. Slim and bright on top, red and fully rounded at the bottom, she went through the first few weeks without a problem. She adjusted her insulin level downward, watched her diet scrupulously, and visited her doctors weekly. Bevacqua had never seen Carla happier, and on a weekday in May when he visited her and walked with her through the park, she reminded him so much of Elaine that he felt as if he were married again. He put his arm around her, led her down the path beneath the highway to the river, and with the sun beating on them from above the towers across the way, they sat on a bench and looked at the sunset. The sky was clear yellow, washing into the river with a brightness that made them squint. A blessing seemed to hover before them, and when Carla talked of her mother, of the care Elaine had always given, saying that he, Bevacqua, had the same kind of tenderness, Bevacqua could only nod helplessly, giving a sappy-throated gurgle.

"Yet with all that," he choked, "with all the tenderness you're used to, you picked a... a..."

"Don't say anything else, Daddy. Mark has very special qualities. If they don't show in obvious ways, that doesn't mean they aren't there."

He squeezed her, agreeing grudgingly that he should remain quiet. Joggers passed, two boys on skateboards, a man on a bicycle whose front wheel was at least five feet high. Its round shape reminded him of Carla's body.

"He has real sweetness, Daddy. He reminds me of Mother — and, despite everything, you. I've never had such personal care."

Bevacqua turned away. "At least he isn't squeamish about children," he said.

"Mark loves them. He would like us to have twenty."

Bevacqua looked at her and shook his head.

At the end of June the baby began to grow more quickly. Bevacqua stared with alarm as Carla's body turned from a pear to an apple, her tiny neck and head a mere twig and leaf above her fully rounded form. She tottered when she walked, her skinny arms and hands a pair of circling birds worrying the baby's passage. Mark strode calmly beside her on the walk whenever they visited from the city. Hand on her elbow, staring at the world with a grim determination, Mark seemed to warn off the prospective grandfather of his child.

"We're not well today," he said, when Bevacqua looked at Carla and asked if something was wrong. "We've entered the critical last three months."

Sonograms had been made, estriol tests taken, amniotic fluids studied. More would be done the following week. The baby appeared to thrive but, Bevacqua feared, perhaps too well. As if in opposition, Carla waned. She became drowsy, irritable, could not sleep at night. Her speech grew sluggish, a sure sign that insulin and sugar levels were not regular. Like a fat alcoholic, she floundered before her father and lover, her skin pale and wet as if she were in a crowded, airless room. At the same time her eyes gleamed as if there were something equally warm and airless going on inside her.

"It's the baby," Mark said with a warning grimace one Sunday afternoon. "It's taking a lot out of her."

The doctor watched more carefully through July and August. Bevacqua knew that at this point the baby would either die or grow too fat to be delivered. Elaine had explained it to him and Carla several times. Either there would be too much acid in her blood, a condition that the baby could not survive, or too much sugar, a condition that Carla might not survive but that, if she did, would create a very large baby. "The growth will either stop or go wild," Elaine had said, as if speaking of a tumor. "About all a doctor and patient can do is be careful. And hope."

In August, Carla took to bed. Mark supervised her nutrition and insulin levels, even injecting her, something Bevacqua would have hired a professional to do. Apart from that, the young man went about his daily work cool and detached, as if Carla were some distant culture he was studying but did not want to disturb. Bevacqua hated the scientific attitude, even as he envied it. He found himself wandering teary-eyed through toy stores and maternity shops during lunch hours. Elaine accompanied him as he ordered a crib, a Bathinette, and little blue and pink sweaters and caps. Once or twice, as he cooked dinner alone at night, he found himself talking to her as if she, not Carla, were the one having the child. "Elaine, I'm in my fifties. In fifteen years I've learned to cook, keep this house clean, and maintain my business. Just as you did. But, with Carla, this is the hardest thing I've ever done."

He would look up from a pile of new baby clothes, or a tomato sauce he was making, and stare into space above the kitchen table. There, as if materializing out of light, silverware, and china, Elaine smiled at him with her hands on her belly, her expression of contentment more a matter of gestation then appetite. She looked young again, healthy, her soft, chatain hair pulled back into an efficient bun. She wore a white smock, rolled up at the sleeves, with the sil-

Fred Misurella

ver horn of a stethoscope poking out of her left breast pocket. Bevacqua found himself talking into it.

"It's not so bad on that side of it all, is it? You look comfortable."

Elaine patted her stomach and shook her head. He smiled, enviously.

"She's our daughter, Elaine. And it, THAT," he pointed to her abdomen, "will be our grandchild. I don't know enough to protect her, as you did."

The specter shook its head and, as if ashamed, looked away. Bevacqua turned down the heat beneath the sauce and stood at the table. Water rumbled in the second pot on the range, and in front of him stiff strands of uncooked spaghetti lay across a bowl. Mark never ate pasta. Too starchy and fattening, he claimed, especially with Parmesan and other cheeses. Grudgingly, Bevacqua took a handful of spaghetti strands, broke them in half, and with a glance for approval at Elaine, dumped them into the boiling water.

No race tomorrow, but he found that as Carla's pregnancy developed he ran farther and farther in each day's workout. Tomorrow, a Saturday, Bevacqua planned to run more than twenty miles. Elaine did not go with him, but he caught glimpses of her here and there behind a tree, a rock, or beyond the crest of a particularly arduous hill. The longer he ran, he thought, the more frequently he saw her. Sometimes he could make her out waiting for him when, turning the final corner from the backroad to his street, he made the last quarter mile sprint to his front door. If he stopped, he wondered, even at this important time of his life, would she no longer be there?

"I don't have the heart to tell you," he said one night, setting the timer of the stove for *al dente*. "But the baby is growing. With all the care we've given, the baby is growing too big. It's all that sugar spilling into her blood."

He looked above the table, hoping for a message, but he

only saw a blank, expressionless face. Elaine tugged at the lapel of her white smock.

"I'm like you," he murmured. "I love life too much — I'm afraid." He turned back to the sauce and, after a shake of his head, stirred it.

They had bought frilly things for Carla, even though Elaine had not dressed well herself. Lace dresses and ribboned bonnets presented their daughter as a darling mannequin modeling for Fragonard. In addition, Carla received music lessons, dance lessons, diction lessons, never complaining, thriving, in fact, because she was gifted.

She learned French at five, did trigonometry at six, and played tennis at seven. Like a bright troll, she skipped happily from one pursuit to the next as if the world were perfect, hardly blinking when her mother and father, blaming themselves for everything, injected her with insulin.

Now she would suffer worse, the limitations of her body descending on her at last with this bundle of fire that threatened to go out of control. When the timer rang, Bevacqua turned off the heat, poured spaghetti and water into the colander, stirring the sauce one more time. Carla would be delivered next week, late in the eighth month, the doctor had said. Her abdomen would be sounded, probed, and poked one final time. If little or nothing went wrong, he would induce labor with the intravenous injection of a chemical. Carla would gasp, breathe, perform Lamaze maneuvers with Mark and her father attending, and, if all went well, deliver a robust, screaming baby who would have a happier, more certain physical life than its mother or grandmother had ever known.

Silent, Bevacqua looked at Elaine. Limitations existed over there as well, apparently. She tugged her lapel as if it were a string, but again her lips did not move. "At best," he whispered, putting his thoughts out loud, "that will be our baby's 'natural' childbirth."

❖

"Hello, Mr. Bevacqua?"

"Yes. Mark?"

"Yes. We're..."

"Is there something wrong with Carla? You've never called before."

"That's because I've never had to call, Mr. Bevacqua. We're going to do it tomorrow. Carla is in the hospital now and will go into delivery tomorrow morning. She asked me to call you so you can be there."

"In the hospital now? Is there — ?"

"Nothing is wrong. They just want to watch her. You'd better get there by eight o'clock."

"I'll be there," Bevacqua said.

A chilly September wind blew across the hood of Bevacqua's car as he drove along the highway in the morning. About a mile and a half from home, he saw a deer lying in the road, its entrails spilling onto the pavement, and almost swerved into a tree to avoid it. He wanted to continue, but he thought of Elaine's sympathy for injured animals and, about 100 yards farther on, stopped. He backed up to the deer and parked on the shoulder of the road.

The legs of the animal twitched as Bevacqua left the car. It was alive, its bloody tongue hanging out as if in afterthought. But it did not seem to breathe. Its eyes roved drunkenly from the road toward Bevacqua and back again. Its antlers were large, too heavy for the little strength it still had, and Bevacqua wondered how it could manage to raise its head.

He did not want to touch the deer, although he knew Elaine would have gone to its side instantly, and he was relieved when another car pulled onto the shoulder and a man stepped out. He carried a rifle.

"A beauty, isn't it? Such a shame. They just don't comprehend the speed of cars."

The man, gray-haired and balding, wore a plaid mackinaw jacket and a pair of baggy corduroy jeans. He leaned back on his heels as he walked. "Must be ten points," he said, standing beside Bevacqua.

"What should we do? I don't know what to do with injured animals." Bevacqua added, "I have a meeting to get to."

The man looked at the deer and shook his head. A semi passed with a roar, its horn tooting, the vibration of its wind and wheels driving Bevacqua back and knocking the buck's head to the pavement.

"Poor thing is miserable," said the man. He bent to touch the deer. With a skitter of its legs, the animal raised its head again and let out a quiet bleat. Cursing, the man took an antler, rested the barrel of his rifle on the animal's shoulder and, just as Bevacqua shouted "No!", pulled the trigger. The report echoed across the road, and Bevacqua turned toward his car, seeing birds fly up from the trees behind it. He jotted the man's license plate number on a pad as he drove away.

It began to rain. Leaves and hail hammered against the windshield as Bevacqua turned onto the interstate going east. At the Delaware Water Gap, the two long hills on either side of the river looked browned, as if a blowtorch had been put to them, and along the roadside, trees wore the frail and bony look of skeletons. The baby would be delivered that morning in a large private hospital that Elaine had practiced in. Bevacqua shivered at the thought of her ghost among them, especially on a day such as this. But when he arrived at the huge hospital lot, parked his car, and rode the elevator to the maternity floor, he felt better for having her near. In a green robe, mask, and cap, Mark stood before him at the delivery room door. He raised his hand, palm out, as Bevacqua took off his coat and hat. "You're late. They've started procedures. They're going to do a Caesarean..."

"Carla..."

"Don't panic, Mr. Bevacqua."

Mark pulled down his mask, revealing the familiar

black-bearded face. A pearl of anger shone in his eyes, and Bevacqua restrained himself as he dropped his coat and hat on a nearby chair.

"This way," Mark said. He led Bevacqua down a corridor to a side room and amid the smell of disinfectant, the ring of bells, and a disturbing urgency of hospital personnel moving in and out the door, handed Bevacqua a gown, a mask, and a cap of his own. "We're going to watch this too," he said. "Unfortunately, it won't be as pretty."

"A caesarean? We're going to watch that?"

Mark nodded, grimly. "Carla wants us there," he said. "The doctor said it's okay. Just scrub up before we go in."

Bevacqua took the gown and slipped it on as if it were an apron. He went to the sink, ran water over his hands, then added soap and built up a lather. He felt weak in the knees but, like a man about to walk to his own execution, tried to separate himself from the event to come. He remembered Elaine resting in his arms in bed at night, tears flowing from her eyes because of a lost patient. He looked at Mark behind him in the mirror and tried to equal his appearance of self-control.

"There will be blood, won't there?"

"A little." Mark nodded. "But Carla won't feel a thing. You and I won't see anything except her face and, when it's delivered, this new Bevacqua-Greenberg baby."

"I don't like hyphenated names."

Mark laughed but said nothing. Bevacqua looked at his hands and rinsed the lather off. He washed again, dried off with a towel, and then, with mask and hat on, followed Mark into the corridor to another door.

"This is it," Mark whispered. He covered his face with the mask and leaned forward. "There will be a barrier — sort of a curtain — between us and the baby. It will be better if you don't look on the other side."

He pushed open the door and Bevacqua shivered as he saw the white, gray, and green delivery room. Carla lay in the center, her body like a huge volcanic mound draped with tapestry. A team of half a dozen or so potential Elaines moved about her, three at a table of sponges, gleaming instruments, and ironed cloths, another near an oxygen table, a fourth, who nodded, looking at the screen of an electrocardiogram machine. She adjusted knobs while a steady beep, beep, beep competed with the clank of instruments, voices, the scuffling of feet.

"Daddy..."

"Baby!"

He ran to Carla, looking to take her hand but finding none available. One lay under the drapery about her, the other was strapped to an arm board, with an intravenous tube attached to her finger.

"You all right, honey?"

"Tingly." She laughed, giggling at Mark, who stood beside Bevacqua. "The anesthesia is moving up my shins."

She laughed again. But Bevacqua saw sweat pouring from her brow and worried. "Are they watching the glucose levels, honey?"

"They're watching," Mark assured him. He moved next to the table and squeezed Carla's shoulder.

"We're going to do it, baby."

"You betcha," she told him.

One of the Elaines stood next to Carla, patted her cheek, and asked how she felt. Carla said that the anesthesia had mounted past her knees.

A man, clearly not Elaine, tall, massive, with the huge fleshy hands of a butcher, stopped near Carla and, after greeting her, looked at some charts.

"The obstetrician," Mark whispered.

"Fathers are both here, I see," the doctor said.

"Yes," Carla said. "That's my dad over there."

He nodded to Bevacqua, then Mark, and turned to the machines beside his patient. He studied the electrocardiograph, asking for blood pressure and glucose levels, and glanced at another man in green who simply nodded back. Turning back to Bevacqua and Mark, the obstetrician said, "You just stay up at that end, away from the action. This will be brief. About fifteen minutes at the most."

"Right," Mark said.

The doctor stared at Bevacqua. "If you feel yourself getting sick, just leave the room. Carla will feel no pain, at most a little pressure from our hands when we break the amniotic sac."

Bevacqua glanced at Carla and saw her, pale, grinning at Mark. He steadied himself on the edge of her table. Carla was tipped to the left and, with her mouth open, staring over the cotton drapery at the obstetrician. He asked for something from the instrument table. Taking it, he lowered it behind the curtain, and Bevacqua closed his eyes as a cold wave of numbness swept over him.

"Oh, I felt it. I felt something that time," Carla shouted.

He opened his eyes, seeing the obstetrician glance at the cardiograph and shake his head. An assistant placed her hands on Carla's abdomen and pressed it. Two other assistants clutched sponges in readiness; a fourth reached into the space behind the drapery and nodded. Staring, Bevacqua had to admit that Carla, mouth closed now, wore the blush of triumph on her face.

"Fine. Looks fine," the obstetrician said to her.

"He looks fine. He looks fine, honey," Mark repeated.

"He?" asked Bevacqua.

There was a scuffle of shoes, a long breath, almost a howl, from Carla's pressed lips, and then a cry. It was primeval. It seemed to have the wind, the rain, and maybe some snow in it. Bevacqua turned and saw the obstetrician holding a baby by its feet. It glistened. Fluid poured from its body, over its genitals, along the umbilical cord. It was a creature, round, pale, gray, with a slightly bluish tint that did not, to Bevacqua at least, look human. One of the assistants put a clamp on the cord, and the obstetrician cut it. "Do you want him now?" he asked, cradling the infant before Carla and cleaning it.

Carla opened her mouth and said nothing. Her lips trembled. "Is that it?" she asked. She looked from Mark to Bevacqua to the doctor, who nodded. "Let Mark hold him first," she whispered. "No. Let my father."

Bevacqua moaned, forcing himself to hold still.

"Do it, Mr. Bevacqua. Do it."

The doctor carefully passed the baby into Bevacqua's trembling hands. Mark stood next to him, patting his shoulder and smiling. The baby was heavy and surprisingly active. Its eyes were closed, but its mouth opened and the sound that came from it was like a scream of anger from the past.

"Hi, honey. Hi, baby." Mark lifted the corner of the blanket and wiped some moisture off the baby's cheek. Bevacqua felt like embracing it, no, squeezing it tightly to his chest. Seeing the blue patches turned to bloody purple and red, he grew faint. He handed the child to Mark and, weakly, reached for Carla's shoulder. Beyond the drape, the obstetrician pulled a large bloody mass from her body. Sickness descended on Bevacqua as a pair of Elaines, wisps of hair quivering beneath the edges of their hairnets, freed Carla's arms and Mark laid the infant on her chest.

After fifteen years, Elaine's voice sounded clearly in his ears: *We did it! We did it, baby! Welcome to life.*

Bevacqua squeezed the father's shoulder, clutched it, and then, letting go, fell slowly, silently, among careful footsteps, to the floor.

RELATIONS

"It is Italian, but it's universal," an ad for a recent Hollywood film says, as if being Italian-American, despite Caruso, Sinatra, Di Maggio, despite Madonna even, somehow lacks significance, or familiarity.

Whatever... It helps put Riccio family life in perspective. We were loud, boisterous, atypical. My father wasn't always a nice, sweet-tempered guy trying to make his family happy. Nor did my mother play Clair to his Cliff, or on the steamier side, the sexy, neurotic mother of some sordid 1950s drama. Instead, there was something odd and operatic between them, and as I try to get a fix on our family relationships, the mystery of my parents' private lives haunts me. Did they love each other? How much? What real feeling lay behind the brio of all their bickering? Listen...

It was a humid summer night in 1954 or so. The three of us sat around in various stages of undress: my father in his baggy shorts and athletic t-shirt, I in socks and a pair of Fruit-of-the-Loom briefs, my mother in a nightgown, her great flabby breasts bulging over the sides, threatening to break the straps and rush us innocents over the threshold into Freudland. She lay next to me in bed, as was her habit, with a newspaper in her hands, leafing through the comics and women's pages, sighing and making occasional comments to my father as he passed back and forth from his desk in the living room to my bedroom.

"What are you doing now, Daniel?" she asked.

"Be quiet, Mary. Just one more line and I've got it."

He was looking up words in my dictionary to help with a crossword puzzle contest in the local newspaper. I lay next to my mother, the sports section propped before me, reading about the problems the Yankees were having. A dim lamp lit the room. Occasionally, through the blinds, an intense flicker of neon-white broke into the yellow and gray shadows surrounding us.

"Rainstorm, damn it. I've got clothes on the line downstairs. Frankie, would you go down and take them in for me?"

"Aw, Ma."

"Come on. Put on your pants and go bring them in. You're a big boy now."

"I am not."

I was ten, maybe eleven.

Frowning, my mother nudged me with her elbow and, sighing, I got up to go. The light from the ceiling gleamed off her salt and pepper hair. As if it were a Klieg lamp, it shone through her nightgown too, outlining shapes and shadows around parts of her that I always scrupulously ignored during our daily passages from dress to undress in each other's not-so-private lives. She put the paper down on her stomach, took off her reading glasses, and stared back at me.

"Come on, Frankie. Get down there before it starts to pour."

Cursing beneath my breath, I threw down the sports section and padded over to my closet. Just then my father entered the room and announced triumphantly that he had finished the final puzzle in the contest and wanted to go out and mail it so he could be first with the correct answer. "Anything you want from downstairs, Mary?" he added, with a smile.

He looked absolutely confident. He had put on his trousers and shoes, apparently ready to walk to the corner in his t-shirt. "Take an umbrella, Daniel," my mother said, "and before you go, take in the wash and hang it on the basement line to dry."

He shook his head. "When I get back. I want to get this into the mail as soon as I can."

"But it'll rain by the time you get back."

"Mary, this is ten thousand dollars I'm waving in my hand. If we win it, I'll buy you a goddamn washer and dryer."

My mother waved her hand and again asked me to go downstairs, but my father, shaking his head, told me to stay inside. As he left, we heard a loud clap of thunder, and in a few seconds rain fell heavily against the windowpanes. I settled into the chair to read more about Berra, Rizzuto, and company; my mother resumed her perusal of the comics. I have always associated newspapers with my mother: Columns of newsprint seem to call to mind somehow the scent and presence of her nearly naked body. As an infant, I listened to her read the funnies to me. As a slightly larger infant, I fondled my mother's breasts, calling the left one Tom, the right one Jerry, and in my play made up games where they chased one another around her chest while she, seemingly oblivious, followed the lives of Dick Tracy, Li'l Abner, Brenda Star, and Dagwood and Blondie, finally closing her eyes and apparently falling asleep.

I often forgot how those cartoon idylls ended, but that night, as I looked at and through her nightgown, I remembered. After dozing, she was seized by bursts of anger, moments when she thrust a newspaper into my hands while she covered the rigid nipples on her breasts. "Stop playing, Frankie. Get out of bed and *do* something with your time."

"But, Mommy, it's —" And meaning to say it was my room, after all, and she had come to visit me, I was surprised to feel her suddenly slapping my face.

"*Read,* I said! Stop bothering me, and let me get my rest. Your father and brothers will be coming home soon, and I have to get them dinner. I spent most of the day cleaning house."

This sort of thing happened many times, but inevitably I returned for more because my mother always seemed to enjoy the play — at first. There was the quiet smile of contentment as I lay next to her, a murmur of dissent as my hands slid beneath the straps, then long moments of silent tolerance as she closed her eyes and I turned her breasts into a Keystone chase: Tom after Jerry, Jerry taking refuge in the mousehole of my mother's armpit. Then the mood snapped, and she sent me running from the room in tears.

Recollecting all that during the rainstorm, I felt ashamed and, as if my clothes were fig leafs, I put on my trousers and shirt and escaped to the living room to read. My father's stand-up desk was open; scraps of paper were scattered about the floor and nearby couch as if they had been scribbled on in a hurry, only to be rejected and cast aside. For the last month and a half, my father had worked on the contest daily. I returned from school to find my books open or missing; when I said hello, I saw him over one of them, smiling with relief because he had just succeeded in finding a word that fit. He checked the answers in the Sunday paper and just the week before had received a letter saying that as a finalist he was required to do a series of tiebreaker acrostics. "These will be more difficult puzzles," the letter warned, "and the first to answer them all correctly will win." That night, I think, he completed the final tiebreaker, and so his haste to get to the post office was understandable.

A tailor by trade, my father was frequently unemployed and had taken to entering contests in an attempt to make a once-in-a-lifetime killing. My mother, a doubter concerning my father, advised him daily to go out and find a regular job. She raised memories of furniture and cars confiscated during the Depression and obstinately reminded my father that those days might come again. He maintained that a regular job wouldn't satisfy him, that this contest wasn't pie-in-the-sky because it depended upon his skill, not luck. He added, "And I've always been pretty good with words, Mary. So have some confidence."

My mother glared. "A good father would support his family first. All you're doing is playing games."

"God damn it, Mary. This is my business. You haven't gone hungry yet, have you?"

"No — but there have been times..."

He waved his hand. "Forget about those other times. That's your trouble; you're always worrying about other times."

These conversations intrigued me, probably because they were talking about life before me. My mother had already spoken to me of evenings in the 1930s when they went with little food, when my sister Rita and my brother Danny had to run to my grandmother's to beg leftovers for dinner, or a period when my father spent a couple of nights in jail. A dining room set had been lost to creditors; the family had come home from a neighborhood movie one Sunday afternoon to find their automobile gone — towed away for lack of payments.

Reversals continued until Pearl Harbor. Through all that long period my father maintained a happy-go-lucky attitude, doing occasional repairs or adjustments for clothing stores, gambling at the local Italian men's club, working as a rental agent, selling a few insurance policies. Until the Japanese struck. Then, as if World War II were fought for our benefit, he found a job as foreman in a clothing factory that manufactured Navy and Marine uniforms. Within months he became a don in the local garment industry, farming out jobs to smaller factories, taking illegal kickbacks from other tailors, and receiving thousands of dollars worth of "gifts" in appreciation every Christmas: toys for us, a family-sized freezer, cases of whisky, shirts by the score, the largest console radio in the neighborhood, and, even after the war was over, a brand new 1946 Nash that my Uncle Ralph drove off the road on the way to my grandmother's on New Year's Day. In fact, this form of patronage kept the family fortunes afloat through most of the Cold War. My mother, guilt-ridden, and less of a long-term optimist than my father, always saw the thirties as returning. For her the war and our illegal riches were threats, and the way to avoid divine retribution remained institutional: a "regular" job, with "regular" hours and pay, which for an irregular man like her husband would be nothing short of prison.

The issue that caught my attention most often during those disputes had to do with my father's manhood. Despite their children, something remained unsettled in my parents' sexual lives. My mother impugned my father's masculinity constantly. She mocked his physical strength, his intelligence, his energy, linking the issue of manhood to money and his lack of a steady job. A "good" father would support his family, according to her. A "real" man would get a permanent job. Simply getting by and having an Italian man's respect among his friends was not enough for her. She brought it up again that water-soaked night.

While I sat quietly in the living room, he mounted the stairs and, with moisture glistening on his bare arms and shoulders, went into the bathroom for a towel. Near adolescence, I had already begun to see the tarnish on him, but he was in such good spirits as he dried himself that something of the man I had worshipped in my infancy came through. "I made it," he said. "I mailed it special delivery. The paper will have it tomorrow morning."

I smiled happily and offered congratulations. In the bedroom, my mother grunted loudly, but after a shuffle of paper, I heard her ask about the wash.

"Don't worry, Mary. I took it in before I left."

A murmur of surprised approval was followed by a suspicious, "Was it dry? Did you put it on the indoor lines?"

"Don't worry. It's taken care of, Mary. I did it for you."

He winked at me, then finished drying himself as she came out of the bedroom to get something from the refrigerator. Rain fell heavily now, so my mother went from room to room obsessively pulling down windows and, as was her fussy habit, wiping the sills dry with a terry cloth towel. My father beamed as he took a part of the newspaper from me, and as he returned to the bedroom my mother asked him again if he had hung the clothes on the indoor line. He hedged a little this time, saying they had been hardly touched by the rain. Then he admitted he left them in a basket by the oil burner.

"The basket," she said. "Why didn't you hang them up?"

He seemed to grit his teeth a moment and then replied, "I told you I left them by the oil burner."

"Stupid! There is no fire in there. This is summer. I told you to put them on the line; why do I have to do everything myself?"

I heard a rustle of paper, and then my father warned her against calling him stupid again. "I put them by the oil burner, I said. They'll be all right."

"But don't you know it's summer, stupid? The oil burner isn't on. Tomorrow you'll be wearing green moldy shorts. They'll match your skin, and I won't want you to touch me..."

I had just begun to lose myself in a sports story again when I heard a crack, then another, and thinking it was lightning, I stood to look out the window. But then I heard my mother shout as the floor of the whole apartment shook with the thunder of my father's footsteps. I ran into the kitchen, saw him holding a rolled up newspaper over her; as I stepped through the door he let it down on her head once, twice, then two or three times more, the last time across her face.

"I told you not to say that," he shouted.

As she raced around the table to hide behind me, I saw a terror in her eyes that I had never encountered before. In an instant she stood behind me, and I understood how quickly the uneven physical balance between them could swing in his favor.

"Wh — Watch out for him, Frankie. He doesn't know what he's doing."

He shoved the table aside. "I *do* know what I'm doing, damn you. Goddamn woman is ruining my whole goddamn life."

He threw the paper at her. But as I stood up to him with, I'm sure, a look of incredulity in my eyes, he stopped, went to the silverware drawer and pulled out a butcher knife.

"Stupid, she calls me. An illiterate. And now you too. I had to teach you both how to read and write."

He waved the knife as if it were a sculptor's tool. As he turned from the counter, my mother shoved me toward him and stepped back into the hall. "He — he — he means it, Frankie. You better watch out for yourself."

More in shock than agreement as I glanced at her, I pulled up in front of him with the blade of the knife nearly touching my chest. My father threw it into the sink, but at that moment my mother called him stupid again, and he snatched it up with a curse. He lunged over my flailing arms as I, just about half his weight, tried to shove him back to the sink and grip the counter to pin him there. I heard a moan; thinking it was my mother, I looked back only to see her teeth clenched together in rage. Then I heard myself pleading with my father to let the knife drop before someone got hurt.

"Hurt? I'll *kill* you if you don't let go!" He pushed against the counter, leaning against me, but just when my hands were about to break free, he screamed. I heard the blade clatter against the enamel sink. He held up his hand, bleeding. "I don't know what I'm doing. I don't. I should have my fingers cut off." I felt his body slacken against the sink and, sickened, I stepped away, avoiding the sight of blood.

"There. There — You've finally shown your son what you're really like, Daniel Riccio. I hope you're happy now."

The sink was covered with scarlet, as if a bucket of paint had been emptied there. As he leaned against the counter he repeated helplessly several times, "I'm insane. They ought to put me in the hospital. That woman is making me do things that even I don't understand." A newspaper slapped against the window beside him, and I turned to see my mother pulling back her arm. She kept wax fruit on the table and, holding a piece of it, she aimed carefully and plunked my father on the head.

"Some man, isn't he? Bullying his wife and son. I've seen him when he's down — when he's peeing in his pants — the coward." Then she turned around, walked into her bedroom and slammed the door with a force that I have remembered through the years because it brought jelly to my limbs. I looked at the blood streaming down my father's hand then hurried to my own room and collapsed onto the bed.

The wound was superficial, physically, requiring nothing more than some wrapping around his left palm. But the psychic wound went deeper. For weeks they didn't talk to one another. My father slinked out of the house without breakfast; my mother grimly went about her household chores. At night we passed hours of silence pursuing our separate tasks. The newspaper sent my father a letter saying he had come in twentieth out of an entry list of thousands, but unfortunately they were giving cash prizes to the first fifteen winners only. As consolation he received a year's subscription to the paper. My mother gloated about that, although as the weeks passed she became more sympathetic. During this time she talked to me of the past and I saw that in some ways my father was as much a puzzle to her as to me. Maybe their relationship was too. He shamed her with rude behavior on many occasions, but just as clearly he had made her love him through a combination of willful independence and helplessness. She spoke of his dapper dress, his reckless way with money when they were young, occasional troubles with the police, and his sudden flare-ups of violence that intrigued her because they alternated with passive, regretful, then amiable behavior. She said there had been instances when men insulted her and my father did nothing but smile meekly and wave them off. She said that once he had struck out then run, pulling her with him, when a man pinched her and three of his friends threatened to beat my father when he protested. He was completely unpredictable: She was ashamed of him sometimes and proud of him at others, especially when the odds were most against him. But when it should have been easy, when the situation was one he should have been able to control, frequently she had to be the more daring of the two.

Once, a year or so after the night of the rainstorm, I saw that happen. The three of us were in a car, driving in town to one of our favorite bakeries. It was another hot night, but this time there was no rain, just the normal muggy air I associated with summer vacation. We were after some special chocolate-filled cannoli, I believe, and as we neared the shop on a busy street, my father saw a parking place in front of it, slowed down, and pulled beside the forward car in order to back in. But as he turned, making the laborious grunts and wheezes that always accompanied his parking motions, he jammed on the brakes, peered out the back window, and, with a quick look at me, said, "What the hell! He's trying to sneak in on us."

"Don't let him do it, Daniel," my mother cried. She craned her neck, shook a fist at the other driver, and leaned out the window to wave him away. My father yanked the wheel, jamming the back part of our car into the front part of the space; the other driver screeched to a halt within centimeters of our rear bumper, and as the horns of the two cars brayed, a crowd gathered on the steps of the bakery. They cringed, I saw, hunching their shoulders as if the impact of the horns had screeching metal in it, reacting as if flesh were torn apart already.

"What the hell you think you're doing, punk?"

My father opened his door and stepped into the street. A bus passed, then a car, followed by a curious teenager on a bicycle.

"You tell him, Daniel," my mother called. "Don't let him get away with anything."

"Up yours, Mac. Get the car out of my space."

From the safety of the back seat, I watched a frail, dark-haired boy, certainly smaller, not much older than I, run up to my father and stop, one finger poking into his stomach. My father towered above him, and I felt an instinctual fear of him myself. But as his eyes met the boy's, I could almost feel my father's weight shift back onto his heels. "Wh — We was there first," he stammered. "I had my signal going before you even arrived."

"It's *my* place, Mac. I don't care whose signal was going."

"Daniel! Don't you take that from him —"

"Ma! — Sh! Let him take care of it."

"And why don't you go out there, Frankie? Why should you let your father face this — this bum out there, alone?"

Leaning over the front seat, pushing forward to give myself room, I put one foot over the running board, just in time to see my father shove the boy's finger from his stomach, then stumble backward when it returned in a fist that crunched against his jaw.

"Daniel! Frankie!"

He was on his back without a second movement, his head crashing to the pavement with a sound that reminded me of porcelain; a frenzied scramble of his legs and feet made him look like a suddenly upended insect.

"Get up, Daniel! Get up!"

My mother was out of the car in an instant. Circling the hood, she whirled her pocketbook in the air, flailing it like a bolo, and caught the young boy by surprise. The leather smashed into his eye, and he reeled. "Hoodlum!" she shouted, Goliath getting even with her David. "It was our space. What right do you have sneaking in on it?"

"I was there first!" he bellowed. His hand flashed up to touch his cheek. "Don't do that again, lady. I'll hit you too. I ain't afraid."

"Daniel! Get on your feet and help me. Frankie, get out of the car!"

But we were both immobilized, one giant praying mantis on his back, the other a grasshopper with all the spring gone from his legs. While my mother turned toward us, the boy jumped into his car, backed out of his half of the space, then screeched around my mother and the crowd as if he were after someone.

"His license plate! Somebody get his license plate number! Did you see it, Frankie?"

I was still in the car, one foot suspended over the pavement as all this occurred. I let the shoe drop and answered with a chirp: "I didn't see a thing. I was too busy watching you and Dad."

"His license? Did anyone see his license plate number?" My mother turned to the crowd and addressed them generally.

"Did anyone see him?" I asked.

Silence, as if a password had been given. While my mother and I looked around the circle of faces for help, my father rose to his knees, stumbled to his feet, and leaned against the car with one hand resting against his cheek. "I'll kill him. I'll murder him," he mumbled. "Got me when my back was turned."

I held his arm to help him into the car, and when he slid behind the wheel, I took my mother's arm and led her back to her seat. "Nobody wants to help?" she said. "Nobody wants to tell me who that boy was?" The crowd remained silent, as if they had just seen something that wasn't real. They began to drift away when my mother appealed to them one by one.

"Nobody knows the guy," one man said, scratching a tattoo on his arm. "He ain't from this neighborhood."

"And no one got his license plate either? Some sympathy you all have."

I slouched into the back seat; before I shut the door, my father had started the engine and began to pull into the street, almost running over one of the bystanders. A young boy came to the window, his thin lips and dark brown eyes giving him an earnest, puppy dog appearance. "You're

Italian, aren't you? You're Danny Riccio's family."

He meant Danny, my older brother.

"That's right. Do you know that — that..." My mother's voice wavered. The incident had been so upsetting, so *surprising* I should say, that even she had trouble finding her usual epithets. With my father leaning pathetically over the wheel, she appealed to the spaniel-like face as if it had a bone to throw back to her.

"Him? — Naw. But we got his face, you see? Me and my buddies will take care of him if he ever shows himself again."

"You know him, you must!"

"You really never saw him before?" I asked.

He held up his hand, pawing at the air as if it were a door he wanted opened. "Swear to God — never. But if he ever comes by, me and my boys will take care of him. We're here every night. We'll keep an eye out." He stared at us, sincerely, but even I could see that tomorrow night would bring another distraction. As he patted my mother's shoulder, shook my hand and, like a doctor, told me to look after my father, he was already turning away. "Be good, eh? Stop by some time and I'll let you know what turned up with that — with that..."

"Hoodlum!" my mother shouted.

"That's right. That's right. And if you don't see me in that bakery doorway, you just ask for Hutch — that's me. Somebody'll tell you where I am."

"Thank you. Thank you very much."

My mother rolled up the window, and a veil seemed to close around our lives. When we got home, it settled over the house in a hush that remained for several days. My father took four or five aspirins and went to bed as if he had a hangover. My mother paced between the kitchen and dining room, keeping the pantry door swinging constantly as she whispered to me and demanded to know why I had not helped my father or her. I felt branded. I leaned against

Fred Misurella

the doorjamb making excuses to myself but imagined an indelible mark of Cain on my forehead. Frightened, certainly, but immobilized by curiosity as well, I had wanted to see my father's actions in public, to know what he was like when he wasn't my father, and, I remember thinking, to get even for the fear I felt since the night he threatened our lives. When my brothers came home they looked at me as if I were a traitor, and since Danny knew Hutch, they drove to the bakery for more information — perhaps, I fantasized, to put out a Riccio vendetta.

They found nothing. They were not heroes or avengers; what's more, neither they nor our family were as much a part of that neighborhood as we thought. Like some mysterious figure of fate, my father's attacker bumped into our lives at a parking space, ruffled our feathers with a single swipe of the hand, then darted away as if propelled by a larger, more forceful power. For a week, while my father remained in bed — out of shame, pain, or both — my brothers cruised the neighborhood around the bakery with two baseball bats and a chain; then they got a lead and drove to two nearby towns in search of the boy. But they found nothing. When my father aroused himself, he went too, vowing "to scare the punk to death," if they found him. After another week they all gave up. My father's jaw looked mumpish on one side, his eye slightly discolored, but when the bruises finally went away, he decided to let his attacker disappear too.

Although it took time for us to see it, the evening showed who should reign in the family. My father still had physical power, he still blew up in anger as before, but we began to regard those outbursts as signs of weakness. The taint in his character, the doubt I sensed the night he turned the knife on himself, now became a distinct discolored spot that, unlike the one around his eye, grew larger as time passed.

Several weeks later, my mother took to bed in a state of exhaustion. Hot flashes caused it, she said. This was the time of her menopause, and she was troubled, but I think there was something else. The week before, Danny had announced his intention to marry, and the following weekend, although six years younger, my other brother, Orie, had done the same. With my sister Rita already married, my father and I were the last ones at home.

"I can't move," my mother said in panic the morning after Orie's announcement. "I can't even lift my hand."

Her eyes were wide and vacant. Her face looked bumpy and pale, as if there were a paste of clay and putty covering it. She could not raise her head. She remained that way for days. My father — with just the right touch of sorrow — cooked for her, fed her in bed, brought her newspapers at lunchtime and read to her. He washed her, helped change her clothing, and spent the evenings in the chair next to the bed talking about things he had done during the day. He carried the tenderness well, and for a while we experienced an unusual sense of calm about the house. Orie and Danny went to work, then met their fiancées at night; I attended school and returned to study in my room; Rita visited from her apartment in New York to help care for my mother; my father took off from a suddenly busy work schedule to be with my mother at meal times. Yet it was short-lived, and the quiet, as seemed inevitable in our family, quickly turned against us. About a month after she took to bed, I heard a high-pitched moan from her bedroom and, thinking it was my mother, I ran to the room only to enter and see my father with his hands covering his face. "I want to help you, Mary. Why can't I help you get better?"

"There, there. You'll be all right. Don't upset yourself, Daniel." She was out of bed, her arms around his shoulders, her finger to her lips as she looked at me and motioned me from the room.

When I returned fifteen minutes later, he lay under the covers, his clothes off, one arm thrown over his eyes. My mother stood in the kitchen brewing chamomile.

"Better?" I said, looking at her as if I suddenly understood everything.

"Frankie, don't take this out on your father. He needs me. It's partially your fault he's in that bed."

"He needs you? So do I; so do we all."

She shook her head.

"Mom, don't let this happen."

She poured tea, nodding but silent.

"It isn't fair — to any of us."

She dumped blossoms and stems from a strainer and wrapped them in a page of Sunday's paper. I inhaled the fruity perfume of chamomile.

"No," she said at last, throwing the rolled-up tea into the garbage. "I guess it isn't, but —"

She shook her head once more.

"Mom — ?"

I waited while she added whisky and honey to the chamomile. Lifting the cup, she closed her eyes and nodded, embracing me. My father called. She smiled. When she entered the bedroom again, she carried the day's comics with her too.

BODY LESSONS

"Go to a doctor, a psychologist then," I tell him. "You want help from *this* world, not the other."

"I want help from *you*, Joey. In the name of our mother and father, you're all I have!"

My brother crosses the room, falling on his knees before me, and kisses my ring. I stare down at the crown of his head, the embarrassingly thinning hair, and no, I am not clairvoyant, but I see the whole torturous course of his future life in front of him: the loss of strength and weight, the diminution of breath and movement, the debilitating freeze. This from a man whose very boyhood personality was defined by strength: the shock of dark black hair, the wiry bursts of movement, and the emotional heat that radiated through the family walls to the world outside. You have seen him and heard him, I am sure. What's more, you have applauded him on his journey from the poor, working class walkways of this neighborhood (a slum I now call my parish) to the small nightclubs and glamorous stages of New York and then, because of a comic imitation of Elvis, to the luminous screens and highways of Los Angeles: a swimming pool, a garage full of sports cars, and a million dollar house!

"Please, Ton-Ton. Stand up. I'm embarrassed."

"I'm sorry, Joey. I know this is a lot to expect from you. But this is my life."

He rises slowly, brushing away the tears. I have seen my brother blond, I have seen him shaved to look completely bald, I have seen him bloated and overweight so that, on screen at any rate, the family resemblance between us is made clear. I have seen him naked, as a corpse on a morgue table. But I have also seen him looking most disturbingly like his younger self, his thick hair black and down around his ears, his voice quick and caustic, and his behavior violent and aggressive as he played a man none of us ever wanted to be: a criminal former Vietnam veteran, a murderer and rapist too involved with power and self to feel regret. There is one scene where my brother, to win a bet, walks up to a young girl standing on a street corner, pulls out a gun and, with a friendly smile and an ironic "thank you," shoots her in the head. Although I assure you his real sins are mild and passive by comparison, I cannot see him apart from that role.

He won an acting award for it, wrote me an awful, gloating letter from Europe telling how, later that month, he went to bed with the beautiful woman who presented the award to him and that next morning, while she slept, he swam nude in the Mediterranean with her sixteen-year-old daughter: "I f---ed her" [he spelled out the word fully] on the rubber raft in the middle of that large round baby blue," he wrote, "and she blew me (you remember that term, Joey? Does it bring back any memories?) in the shade of the cabana just a few minutes later. Oh, it's great to be young, to love, to have it all!"

And to lose it, too.

❖

"Hey, Joey. Come over here. I want your opinion."

My mother and I stood in the basement; a white tablecloth covered the huge plywood board (on saw horses) around which we would gather that afternoon for family dinner. The coconut my father had painted and decorated to carry the likeness of a cannibal had been dusted; drawings of Jesus, along with those of movie stars, hung on the walls. A small white Christmas tree lit up the bookshelves in the corner, and the big tree, a fir surrounded with gifts, stood in the living room by the fireplace. Meanwhile, a console phonograph piped out the recorded voice of my idol, Mario Lanza, singing "Ave Maria."

"Get away from those sweets, Joey. Come taste this for me."

Assorted pastries covered the table: tollhouse cookies, banana cake in the shape of Our Virgin Mother's head (aqua-tinted dye in the icing colored her robe and eyes), a large, three-layered chocolate cake, and three or four fruit pies. My mother stood apart from them, in a coal bin my father had hammered, plumbed and stretched into a second kitchen several years before. With guests expected in addition to family, she had decided to cook down here to keep the upstairs apartment clean. A large pot of tomato sauce simmered on the stove, the heat slowly floating and revolving sausage, meatballs, and *bragioli* in the liquid. On the table and stove lay the materials of the main dish for the day: My mother's meat lasagna.

"Here, Joey. I want your opinion. Tell me if this needs anything more."

My mother motioned to a huge bowl of ricotta, mixed with eggs, parsley, basil (in our dialect we called it *vasnigol*) and, of course, Romano cheese.

"Mmmm. Delicious. Maybe it needs a little more salt."

My mother added some cheese from a jarful I had grated earlier. Then she urged me to try the sauce. The fumes were aromatic, almost like incense. After I winked, giving the sauce my okay while suggesting a little more pepper and Romano, she drained the boiled noodles and began to lay out two panfuls of dinner.

"Are Maria and Vinnie coming on time this year?" I asked.

She smiled. "I told them around two o'clock. But you know, with traffic through New York, that could mean three or four."

I giggled. My sister and her husband lived in Brooklyn and perhaps because of distance, more likely because of Vinnie's tendency to sleep late on holidays, they always arrived late for family meals. "We'll all be hungry by the time they come," I said, "especially me."

My mother smiled again, and began to pile up lasagna noodles. I always saw her as a mason at these moments: First a layer of lasagna on the bottom, a ladleful of odoriferous tomato sauce, then a big helping of the ricotta cheese mix and chopped meat, followed by another layer of noodles. She had stout arms. Although she carried a spatula instead of a trowel, she proceeded with such care and deliberation that I frequently imagined a wide brick wall going up instead of pasta.

"I'm almost ready for the chickens," she said. "Do you want to clean them?"

I nodded, but reluctantly. Despite their rich, buttery flavor, I had little stomach for chickens in those days. The morning before I had driven to the market with my father and as usual he bought the chickens freshly killed. He had held my hand as we entered and led me to the cages of birds so that I could pick the ones I fancied. The smell and sound of the place offended me, but nothing like my anxious feeling when I pointed to a chicken, saying, "That one!" and in a split second, it seemed, the proprietor yanked it from the cage, twisted its neck with a gap-toothed smile, and tossed it lifeless onto the counter to be plucked and cleaned.

"Life comes out of death," my father had whispered after one of those visits, and I always remembered that whenever we went to the market. I didn't like the idea in those days (although, with my eating, I live by it now), and neither did the chickens: they fought back frequently. I remember once or twice seeing talons imbedded in the back of the proprietor's hand or finger. I felt sickened, and I never could eat fowl until later, when I was older, and we picked it cut up from a supermarket counter.

But I could not retreat from such basic revulsion that Christmas morning. Three huge birds lay on a table near the sink, and, after turning on the faucet, I began to wash them, one by one. Mercifully, the proprietor had cut their heads off, so I turned each one upside down, letting the water run into the pelvic cavity until it gushed out the neck end. This was alive just yesterday, I knew, until I pointed to it. Gingerly, as if reaching into a hornets' nest of revenge, I stuck my hand into the body and raked out the organs with my fingers. Heart, lungs, kidneys: a miniature biology lesson; and, ten or eleven as I was, it fed my growing curiosity about the body. Is this the way I am inside? I wondered. Or my mother? And the soul: If the bird had one, would I pull it out with the gizzard? I'd already asked my mother these questions in more guarded phrasing of course, but with no satisfactory answers. "You'll learn later," she told me once, "when you grow up. You're too young to think about it now."

My father, having already whispered that sentence about life feeding on death, agreed with her.

I accepted their answers, despite my growing sensitivity to differences between my mother's body and my own, our bodies and the chickens', despite thoughts I was beginning to have about character, morality, and soul. I really believed my parents, that as I grew older I would learn. From the way they, especially my father, talked, life was a kind of puzzling magic show that I had to accept on faith, like religion. I assumed my moment of illumination would occur one day in the future, in a sudden, but strictly measured, glow. Shall I add the obvious? — Despite my age, my priestly clothes, and my confessional experience, I still feel I am standing in the dark.

"You want these cut up now, Ma?" I asked.

"Of course, you know we eat them that way. We're having *cacciatore*."

"Ych-ch-ch."

My mother frowned. "If you don't want to cut them, I'll do it myself, Joey. As soon as I finish the lasagna — and cut the potatoes, and peel the onions; and then make the mushroom sauce you love."

She looked severe for a moment. With red-faced effort, she lifted the large pan of lasagna and struggled with it to the stove. This was a wall of bricks, remember, not a pan of noodles. A well-intentioned son, I reacted accordingly.

"Ma, Ma, I'll do that! It's too heavy for you." But she had it at the stove already, and watched, contemptuously, while I carried the second, lighter one from the table.

"I'm not eating *cacciatore* today," I told her, despite her condescending look. "I'll clean this stuff, but I refuse to eat any."

My mother grabbed a knife from the stove, used her hip to shove me away from the sink, and laughing while calling me a sissy, started to hack at one of the birds herself.

"Ma, come on, stop. Let me do it."

"You can't!" She stuck the knife into the joint of the thigh and, leaning all her body weight into it, severed the leg. "I want you to try to eat chicken this afternoon," she said. "It's good for you. You have to understand blood. And accept it. Now peel the potatoes."

"I *never* eat chicken, Ma, whether I cut it or not. It makes me sick!"

"Joey, it's not the chicken, it's your head. Go peel the potatoes. Your father's doing the mushrooms upstairs, and I'll do the onions when I finish these."

"But I *want* to do the chickens!" I cried. She had a broad back, a sturdy, mason's shoulders, yet my mother was my mother, and there was something that made me think of her as delicate. It wasn't proper for her to be cutting into all that bone and flesh.

"*Peel* the potatoes," she said, leaning into another joint. "You can do the chickens when you get older; it won't turn an adult person's stomach."

"All right," I said, "but I still won't touch any today."

I brought the bag of potatoes to the table, started trimming them. A few minutes later my father came down with a bowl of cleaned mushrooms. After placing them in a pot on the stove, he began helping me. It amazes me to think about those mornings now; my father relished everything about chicken — necks, organs, even the "Pope's Nose," as he called the anus — but apparently he too had no stomach for cutting into one uncooked. "Anna," he would say to my mother, "if I do the vegetables, will you take care of the fowl?" She said she would, but always with a hint of scorn in her voice, as if it were something a father of boys should never refuse. That day he said, "After the potatoes, Anna, is there anything else?"

"Is the *antipasto* set?"

He nodded. "Are you sure you can manage the rest?"

She shrugged and smiled. "Carmine and Anthony will be here. They can help if I need it. Go ahead."

My father winked at me and grinned. By this time we had peeled nearly twenty potatoes; with about five more we would be finished. "You want to go with me?" he asked. "Carmine thinks he's too grown up to visit family this year."

"I don't know, Dad. Maybe not."

I shrugged and turned away, hoping I could soften his disappointment. Christmas morning visits to his family were my father's favorite holiday tradition; he looked forward to them every year while his sons got increasingly less interested. He would visit most of my aunts and uncles, drink a glass of wine or whisky with each, and then visit several cousins. He normally took my brother Carmine and me along (my younger brother Ton-Ton stayed home to practice his guitar), but at sixteen Carmine evidently had had enough.

"You'll get some gifts. Your Aunt Sarah and Uncle Ralph always have something under the tree. And my cousin Eddie is always good for a couple of bucks."

"I don't know, Dad."

"It's Christmas. Come on."

But my fear of being shown off, especially alone, was

very strong. I was bashful and, unlike Carmine, spoke Italian poorly; what's more, I was self-conscious among the Grassos and never felt I belonged. Besides, the real main event of the day was home, with my mother, the pasta, and the birds. I wanted to be with them.

"You don't need me, Ma?" I asked, hoping she did. But when my mother shook her head, and my father genuinely pleaded with his eyes, I really had no choice.

"Alright, alright," I said, "if you want me to."

"If I want you to!" My father pounded my back. "Good boy, Joey!"

We finished the potatoes quickly and set them on the stove. Then we put on our coats — new ones that my father, a tailor, had made for the season — and left a short time later. The morning was cold, crisp, sunny, perfect for the holiday. We drove across town, visiting relatives one by one, and, since several cousins were spending the day together, didn't take much time. Traditionally, the last two visits were to my Grandmother Grasso's house and then to my father's cousin Eddie. As usual the visit to my grandmother's took an hour, and just as we were about to leave that day, she turned to me, pulled a roll of bills from a refrigerator drawer, and gave me two dollars, then two more each for Carmine and Ton-Ton. "Merry Christmas, happy new year, to you and your brothers," she said. Barely pronouncing the words in English, she caressed my cheek.

"*Grazie, Nonna. Buon natale.*"

She rubbed my head and smiled at my Italian. My father had rehearsed it with me in the car on the way here from my Aunt Sarah's, and when I looked now, I saw him red-faced and beaming. I stood to kiss her, but my grandmother pulled her head away abruptly. "Cold, a cold," she said, placing two fingers to her mouth. "One kiss enough. *Buon natale.*"

I thanked her again, in English this time, and after a brief, smiling exchange with her in dialect, my father finished his whisky and led me out the door.

We arrived at Eddie Grasso's between noon and one o'clock. A little drunk by this time, my father insisted that we stay an hour or two, until it was time for dinner. I minded, hungry, jealous of Carmine and Ton-Ton, wondering if we would be later than even Maria and Vinnie. But it did no good to argue. For my father, the visits to Eddie were the most interesting part of the Christmas journeys because they reminded him of his youth. For me they were the most troubling because they reminded me of my future. Eddie Grasso was a sweet, gentle man, but fat, grandly fat, a seemingly contented person who, my father said, weighed over four hundred pounds. There were nasty rumors about him in the family: that he lacked sexual parts, that he liked boys, worse, that there was something strange going on between him and his sister. The rumors made my father angry, but until years later I never understood why. Eddie had a bald head, bulbous, hanging dewlaps for jowls, a fat neck that I've seen as thick only on statues of Popes or Cardinals in Rome, and a drape of chins that hung from his mouth and chest as if they were chiseled. He smiled easily, however, especially at my father, and said, "Hiya, Anthony, *Buon Natale*," with such a high voice and joyous grin on his face that you would have thought he was an angel. And when he saw me slide from behind my father's legs, Eddie reached out like an old *compare* to grasp my hand. My fingers sank into the bottomless softness of his palms.

"*Madonna*, Anthony, he's even bigger than last year. Still has the skinny arms though." He studied me carefully, as if I were a mirror, and ran his fingers over his bulging, womanly chest. I smiled and, silent, pulled away.

"He's going to be like you, Eddie. Another four hundred pounder — at least. You know he wears a size thirty-eight coat already?"

"Yeah?" And, as on every other Christmas morning, when he learned my weight or suit size, Eddie Grasso laughed, took out a roll of bills, and, peeling off three or four as if they were leaves of a magnificently buttered artichoke, handed them to me with hardy season's greetings. By that time his sister Margaret, a slim, kindly woman who, it was said, had wasted her youth taking care of her brother, entered the kitchen with a platter of *dadals* — honey-covered pastries I adored — and sat me down to them with a glass of milk and a pile of napkins.

At that point, my father and Eddie began to drink. My father chose scotch; Eddie, as always, had beer. They talked about old times, and as I dreamily fingered and chewed a dozen or so *dadals*, a part of me receded into the background — not to listen to language or dialect, as at my grandmother's house, but to study Eddie Grasso himself: his body, its folds, the huge chunks of flesh dangling from his limbs. I remember looking at his thighs and wondering, as if he were a capon to be cleaned, how he looked between them. Was what they said about him true? Could he function normally, as a man? Beyond that, could a soul find room inside that copious belly? Finally, and most importantly, on Judgment Day, when the good were supposed to receive their bodies in perfect condition, as Monsignor Cavallo often told us, would he be our Eddie still — overweight, hobbling, holding on to tables and chairs just to make a visit to the toilet? Like his sister, he never socialized, hardly went out of the house except for church and work; and as far as I knew his only entertainment was what he saw before him as food. I rarely saw him eat a meal though; the only thing he consumed during Christmas visits were a few of those *dadals* and a couple of quarts of beer. In fact, my father, who had grown up with him, used to tell me that Eddie didn't eat much at all.

"Not eat much! Why doesn't he lose weight then?" I asked.

"He can't," my father said, as if the answer were obvious.

I looked at him, cringing, feeling something ominous in the words, as well as the pit of my stomach — and soul.

"*Can't* lose weight? Really?"

"Glands," my father said. "He was born that way."

He lowered his eyes and stared at my own burgeoning belly and hips. Corpulent himself, he was nowhere near his cousin's size nor the one I would eventually become. My father went on to say, sadly, that Eddie's weight was due to inherited glandular problems about which doctors had told the family there was nothing they could do.

"Nothing? Eddie *has* to look and move that way?"

My father smiled. "You think he *wants* to be that big, Joey? It's good for his voice, maybe, but nothing else. Not his health — and especially not his love life."

I looked at him and said nothing. Yes, Eddie was a professional singer, as I wanted to be in those days, not a *castrato*, but a tenor with a note so youthful it was abnormal, so high and light that it would put Pavarotti or Domingo, and some contraltos, to shame. Still, my father's comment brought a considerable charge of despair into my aching, spiritual heart. Ambitious as I was, longing for a sign that I was chosen, I secretly hoped my weight — or the increase of it — would turn out to be a glandular problem too, God's biological method of testing the strength of my soul, even as He augmented my voice. I never seemed to consume more than anyone else, yet I was the only one in the family grossly out of proportion. My older brother Carmine was broad but tall; my younger brother, Ton-Ton, was muscular but short; my sister Maria was slim, although admittedly she watched how much she ate. And my parents, stomachs blossoming, cheeks bulging, shoulders and arms spreading, always seemed, miraculously, majestically, just right, at least in relation to Eddie. Unfortunately it was I, just learning about saints, girls, filthy jokes, and operatic music in our parish's Catholic school, who for some reason never looked quite normal. I, that is, and Eddie. For a reason always understood but never discussed, we were, by individual paths, different from the others, on a special mission that included food, drink, music, and, perhaps, God, but never women. And I would learn the reason, if my parents were right, as I passed through a magical period — that is, as I "grew up," as my mother put it, and became a man.

"Does he *ever* go out, Dad?" I asked, wondering about the occasions of sin and adolescence, when, as the nuns told me, my voice would crack and other flaws would assert themselves beneath my clothes. "Does he always sit in that same chair in the kitchen?"

"You know, Joey. He goes out sometimes, to work or church, to sing and stuff. But they make him pay double fare in movies and on buses."

"*Double* fare?"

My father grinned. "He takes up two seats, Joey. If you become a priest or a famous singer, maybe they'll let you get away for free."

My father looked at me, smiling. Then he responded to the concern I must have betrayed on my face. "Don't worry, Joey. You're growing, but not that big. Your mother and I won't let you."

"But maybe you can't stop me — or maybe I don't want to stop myself!"

"Don't want to! Why? Are you crazy?"

"Because sometimes I do want to get fatter! I don't know why. If it would make me sing better, or have a better life, I'd do it. I *do* do it! That's why I'm so big." I looked down at my stomach, poking a roll of flesh on my side. "Maybe fat is who I am!"

He shook his head, grinning. "Baby fat is who you are, Joey. As you grow up, you'll lose the weight; it's a matter of time."

"Time? But I *always* eat too much, Dad! How will time change that?"

My father shrugged, more serious. "You'll see. It's nature. As you grow up, you'll see it happen."

My father thought that girls, or my boyish interest in

them, would gradually occupy my mind more than food. My mother agreed. Girls would lead me to exercise, diet, maybe abandon my religious ambitions and take up popular, possibly lucrative, American music like Ton-Ton. Yet even in the context of this man-to-man talk my father wouldn't directly mention sex or money that day. He looked at me blankly, shrugged again and muttered, "Your appetite will change. Don't worry."

In those terms, I still haven't grown up, I think, and I wish, God rest their souls, I could tell both my parents that today. I haven't grown up in the sense of crossing a certain line and being there. As my parents conceived of it, I think, there would be a break-in, or initiation, period of some kind. Maturity was simply a matter of waiting my turn, passing through years, maybe attending a certain number of classes, parties, and masses. Or even singing certain songs. As my father put it that Christmas morning, "Eddie is just a voice, a biological mistake that never developed or changed. We love him, but he is not your future or fate." Except for his singing, I might have answered but only wished, whose silver, expressive quality sounded purer to me every day.

When Eddie died some years later, around 1960, and I saw him filling, almost over-filling his coffin, I could not help placing myself and my ambitions in there with him. He had died of a heart attack while singing in the shower one morning, then had lain for hours on the bathroom floor until his sister Margaret came home and found him, finally, breathless. Yet, despite the awful circumstances of his death, his voice had been lighter, purer, and conversely stronger in the last few minutes, his neighbors told us, than it had ever been. By then I knew I could never equal him, so when his sister asked me to sing for him at the funeral mass a few days later, I chose something simple and obvious, pieces he had performed often on Sundays, without even trying: "Pater Noster" and "Ave Maria."

However, as I stood beside the open coffin and tried to equal him, I couldn't control myself or my singing. I cried and the words of the song tumbled out off key as I looked to find some trace of change in Eddie's face, the slightest sign that the sweet final moments of music had brought him understanding. But his mouth and eyes were shut, his jowls hung stiffly down his neck, his wrinkled brow and naked head gave him the look of a wayward, defrocked monk — a quiet, innocent one who had never got beyond faith to comprehension.

He died just before Christmas, and when my father and I drove home from the visit with Eddie that year, my mother and brothers rode with us, and we all felt uncomfortably close to the coffin. My father steered badly, veering close to cars, blundering through red lights as he muttered comments and prayed or whispered constantly to himself. In the back seat Carmine stared at his feet and strummed an imaginary guitar, while the irrepressible Ton-Ton lip-synced a popular song in silence. My mother stared grimly at the road and I, worried about size and voice and what they would both mean for the quality of my life, especially now that Eddie was gone, did nothing but fold and unfold my hands.

We did not soon get over it. For days I could not look at food or the scene of the crèche under the family Christmas tree. Carmine went out frequently, and Ton-Ton, unhappy with the quiet mood of the house, stayed in his room and played Elvis Presley records over and over. As usual, I stayed with my mother. She helped to free me, talking about Eddie and eating as she tried to cook her self and her family back to assimilation. By contrast, my father sat near the fireplace, reading newspapers and brooding over the headlines for weeks.

To my mother I said, "Dad's taking it pretty hard. I didn't know he would be bothered so much."

She waved her hand. "Eddie's close, family." Then, frowning, she shook her head, and for a moment I saw something light her eyes.

"Your dad's just not used to these things," she said, handing me a homemade cookie from the stove. Then oddly, as if she were talking about cutting chickens: "He's just not seen enough yet."

She had lost her mother, father, and two older brothers to a flu epidemic when she was young. And another brother, Joseph Affamati, whose namesake I am, had died, a few years before I was born, fighting on the beaches of Normandy. Used to loss, she continued about her work, possessing an admirable, almost cheerful, resolve about bereavement and the loss of loved ones. My father, with both parents and a full family surrounding him, acted more troubled, confusing me because he let my mother express the stoic attitudes.

She is the one, in fact, who taught me: "Go about your business, Joey: clean, cook, eat. Above all, practice singing. Beauty overcomes death. It's the little, daily things that help you see that."

❖

There are several photographs from those Christmas mornings, a few of my father and me after our visits to Eddie and the rest of the Grasso family. It is interesting to see the differences between my father and me. The picture I remember most was taken by Ton-Ton, who had received a camera with a flash attachment that morning. He snapped it just as we returned from Eddie Grasso's. Standing in front of our family car, my father and I wear our new wool coats: his a two-toned brown and tan, mine a green and gray oatmeal tweed. My father's arm rests on my shoulders, and he smiles exuberantly, with contented cheer, because as yet death has not struck our holiday. His hair is brushed back from his forehead, his mustache is full and trim, his cheeks are pink and fleshy with the optimism of a long and happy morning. The picture has been hand-tinted, I believe, and we both look a little too healthy, a little too briskly painted by the weather.

My mouth is open, in mock song I remember, with the breath just bubbling from my lips. I wear a cap as well as the coat, earmuffs lifted off my ears, the peak scrupulously pointing skyward (along with my breath), as if it were a black biretta and I already a laughable singing priest. I do *not* smile or laugh as I sing, however, much as I might today. Instead, like Ton-Ton in countless motion pictures, I greet the camera with a scowl, I thrust my left foot forward and, a ready fighter, hold my hands above my rounded belly, clenched into fists.

I was my mother's son in that. Looking at the picture now with my poor sick brother (and, finally, giving him absolution), I perceive myself defending against the camera's eye.

"*Smile, Joey, you're on Candid Camera,*" Ton-Ton said, pointing a finger at me.

I saw appetite, not fire or ice, as dangerous. Despite my song, I heard something unknown and watchful advancing toward us; for the moment of the flash, I prepared to beat it off with all my strength.

FLAMES

Elle avait eu, comme une autre, son histoire d'amour.
—Flaubert

Years afterward, Felicia returned to Saxton, but only because she had nowhere else to go. At a counselor's suggestion, she entered college and took a job as a guard in the shopping mall at Christmas. Two semesters afterward, scoring first or second in all her written college examinations, she applied to the county police academy — again at the counselor's suggestion — was accepted, and in a year and a half suited up as Saxton's (and the county's) first woman officer. "A 'Feliciatous' Achievement," said the headlines in the local newspaper. A front-page article pointed out that in returning to Saxton, she had returned to the scene of a tragedy: the loss of her best friend to fire.

Felicitous or not, certain things about Felicia did not make the front page: a rookie, she worked the graveyard shift alone; hard-working, but not a very graceful athlete, she felt out of place in her uniform and, therefore, never quite real; finally, men, especially large, especially beer-bellied, drunken men, tried to test her strength as a joke and sometimes did fairly well. But through a combination of skill, stubbornness, and clever strategy (her best asset), she managed to gain respect, never completely losing confidence in her abilities, mainly because of an evening's encounter with Octavio Marx, the mayor's delinquent son.

"Ox" his friends called him. His broad back and weight-lifter's arms and shoulders fit the young man as if he had grown into his nickname. Felicia — Officer Felicia Potenza now — met Ox while driving down Main Street in Sexton during her second week of solo cruiser patrol. Midnight. A man stumbled suddenly from the curb, hit the blacktop not twenty feet in front of her, then, on hands and knees, stared into the cruiser's oncoming lights as if he were stunned. He raised his arms, hunched his shoulders, and then, to her never-ending surprise as she bore down on the brakes, bellowed. Felicia jerked the wheel to the right, fought for control, the tires slid and screeched to a stop against the curb. Cautiously, she opened the cruiser door and peered out.

"M-m-oooo," she heard. "M-m-oooo-ooo."

"Hey, get up there! You're going to hurt yourself!"

A series of hiccups and grunts greeted her, and then a chorus of giggles and oinks ripped the air from the opposite sidewalk. Something huge and round clanged on the cruiser's hood and then bounced to the pavement with a liquid squish.

"Hey, Officer ... Lady, watcha gonna do?"

In the beam of her flashlight, Felicia spotted a pumpkin, split, its seeds glittering like silver beads against the blacktop. A young woman in an open-necked shirt stood on the opposite side of the roadway and, like a phantom escaped from a comic strip, a hooded figure stared at her from the passenger side of the cruiser. More than ridicule and Halloween fun, she thought. Drugs, alcohol, or something worse clouded the October night.

She radioed the station for backup, then shouted, in as low a register as she could muster, "On your feet!" while stepping out of the cruiser. The man on fours mooed louder, rose to his haunches, and, gracefully, with a slow, not quite ludicrous shift of his buttocks mid-motion, charged Felicia, his fingers extending from his forehead as if they were a pair of horns.

"Stop! Stop, I said!"

She sidestepped at the last instant as the man's fingers and head bruised the flesh on her hip. Stumbling, she kept her feet by holding onto the cruiser's aerial. Fingers gored more deeply on the second pass, and this time in a switch of positions so swift it struck her as illogical, Felicia found herself on her seat, her teeth jarred with the force of the fall, her feet sliding off the back of a second body resting on all fours. In the bleak haze of the street lamp she saw the girl who had stood on the curb: long-nosed, four-legged, attractive, feral now — a fox — and like a fox, Felicia thought, cruel.

"Got you, Fat Ass!"

Felicia rolled to her knees quickly, and as the bull came at her again, dodged, like a matador, slapped him with her hand and lowered her billy club across his shoulders several times. She leaped to her feet.

"Ow! Don't do that!" he cried, feigning injury as he turned.

"Up against the car! You, too! Against the car!"

The girl, still on all fours, shook her long, dark hair, glared at Felicia and, snarling, bit her leg. The hooded phantom now stood next to the bull; together, they came from behind, shoving to help the girl trip Felicia again. She stabbed the bull's flanks with the billy club and swung at the phantom, bruising his thigh and, on a second swing, ticking the end of his hood. The three struggled for a few moments. A cruiser pulled to the curb just as Felicia and billy club had bull and phantom cowering against the car. Then a fellow officer, Max Gallardi, stepped from the cruiser, pulled the young girl to her feet, and, with a curse, motioned the others to be quiet.

"Hands off, you pig! Get your hands off me!" the girl shouted. She shook her arm free. In the glare of the headlights, Felicia saw a flash of her teeth and cringed at Max's scream.

"Ow! Bitch! You fucking bitch! Stand over there!"

Max shoved the girl at his cruiser, crushing her against the fender with his club placed against her neck. "There may be another somewhere," he whispered. "Did you look?"

Fred Misurella

Felicia swung her searchlight to the curb, beyond that into some bushes. No one. She pulled off the phantom's hood and, seeing the face, looked at Max. He leaned against the cruiser and groaned.

"Oh, Christ, you two again. You ought to be ashamed."

The young men said nothing. The girl went rigid, her eyes blank, her hands shifting on the cruiser's body as if she were clutching for a rope. Max still held her pinioned by the neck, but with his hands now. And, to Felicia at least, he pressed less.

"Ox, your father's going to be mad as hell," Max said. "If you were my kid, I'd throw you out of the goddamn house."

"M-m-ooo!" Ox cried. "M-ooo, hoo, hoo!"

In the beam of her light, Felicia spied a round, stupid grin. Dark, curly hair, dull, empty eyes, an expression distinctly unlike his father's. "Alcohol," she thought. And probably something else. A car passed. When Ox and the Phantom mooed again, Max turned to the girl in disgust.

"They make you happy, heh? What is *your* father going to think?"

The girl wrenched away and, for the barest, briefest instant, looked at Felicia in pain. Slight on top, with long, muscular legs, she wore sneakers and jeans, and a dirty checkered shirt, unbuttoned down to her bra. Turning on Max suddenly, she spit at him. "I'm with them because I want to be, Pig-face. Mind your business."

Max raised his free hand to slap her. Felicia grabbed his wrist. "Max! No!"

With a breath, he stiffened, let his hand drop to his side, and cursed, loudly. He took out a handkerchief and wiped his face with one hand still on the girl. At that moment, Felicia felt happy about herself and her work. Together she and Max put the men in the rear seat of Max's cruiser and, with the girl next to Felicia in hers, they drove to the station. After several phone calls, she and Max booked all three as minors and checked for drugs. As Felicia suspected, they found alcohol, with traces of other things — not recorded — mixed in.

❖

In memory, two incidents often play the same, Felicia's grief counselor told her, although years and circumstances separate them. If life is difficult, memory may be worse, not allowing us to move on, start over, learn; not allowing us the luxury of sequence and progression, because, and this is true for Felicia Potenza's Saxton recently, in memory all time is now. ...

Michele lives. Together they sleep — beautifully, peacefully, lovingly, yet, as they have dreamed, independently. Wind blows, clouds gather, a mixture of air, heat, and current swirl into a point. On this particular night the point condenses, shrinks almost to the state of non-existence, and then in one improbable moment expands as though it were breath, gasps, and seeks release. Lightning flashes, its jagged edge of sky striking a power line near the transformer of their trailer. A rush of sparks and cracks awakens her (as it would in the middle of the night for years). Felicia dives through the door of their bedroom and, again and again, sure she sees and hears Michele running and calling behind her, runs as hard as she can. Across the road, when she turns, looks back to see the propane tank explode (amebas of light, yellow, white, and orange, flash and disappear, "Beautiful, really," she tells the counselor), Felicia hears nothing else. Worse, she sees no running figure behind her. Neighbors — and in her dreams occasionally, Max Gallardi or Octavio Marx — hold her, screaming, back. By the time the fire truck arrives home is a melted mass of plastic, metal, and rubber, the strange burning odor of wood and something else more sinister, animal, hanging in the air. "Smoky," is all she can say about it afterward to the counselor.

Odor becomes memory. Memory spreads, thickens, fouls itself, gathers weight, transforming into more than simple recollection, more than Michele even; like a perfume of emotion and thought, it carries the substance of Felicia's secret self, gathering a second incident in Saxton, lighter, comic ("mere Halloween antics" of Ox, the Phantom, and a cowgirl, as the paper describes them), yet changing the universe of its shape: nightmare becomes dream again, dread becomes laughable frisson, distance becomes a near presence.

Love. Indeed, Felicia is happy to be herself, and at last glad to be a policewoman, she tells her counselor.

❖

"She's a fox, just like my daughter," Felicia's cousin Nick said when he saw her picture. "But you have to watch her."

Six months passed. At 17, this same girl, this presence, Sharon, became a staff photographer for *The Weekly Times,* the Saxton town paper. In an article printed on the back page, her father, Vincent Barns, a geography professor at Saxton College, says that Sharon became a photographer because Patrolman Felicia Potenza took a motherly interest in her. Felicia observed his shame when he picked up his daughter at the station on the night of her arrest. He pleaded with Max and the Chief to help the girl, but not till Felicia suggested herself that she might attempt something for Sharon — and, by the way, for Ox — did Barns seem satisfied. His beard, his thinning hair, the sorrowful expression of his mouth gave him a proud look, but Felicia saw deep pain in his large brown eyes that mirrored his daughter's. They both brought to mind darker, deeper images than Felicia liked to think about but knew too intimately (in her dreams, at least).

A widower, Barns lost his wife at a very early age and raised Sharon himself. He had done his best, Max Gallardi insisted, with professional help, therapists, and many counselors. Yet the girl turned out badly and, Max thought, was only headed for worse, mainly because of Ox and the Phantom. But in the weeks that followed their first meeting, Felicia kept Sharon busy without them, encouraging her interest in hiking and photography, taking her for nature walks in the mountains surrounding town.

"Thanks," Sharon said, as they stood together on the highest peak above Saxton and watched a new comet gleam in the sunset.

"No, thank *you*," Felicia said. "I'm enjoying it. This is a rare sight, but it's rarer still for two people to fall together so easily."

Sharon took the shot, developed it, and brought it to *The Weekly Times*. In a few days, she saw her work, and name, in print.

Felicia took Sharon to the Saxton detox center near College Hill. They sat on a bench, with the sun behind them, and observed the dazed, baggy-pants mixture of junkies, alcoholics, and crack heads that strolled on the grounds, tossed Frisbees, or clipped and pruned the manicured gardens. Sharon looked startled, even frightened, when one of the patients turned out to be a friend from school.

"Jesus, Felicia. Is this where I'm headed? Is there any hope?"

Felicia patted her shoulder and smiled. "There are always other ways. That's what these places do — they help you find other paths. With hope."

"I'm a bad one," Sharon said, frowning at a young man stumbling along the walkway. He muttered to himself, his eyes vacant, his chin hanging, his smile absolutely painted.

"So was I," Felicia said. "Even worse. But I changed. We all change. You can, too."

Sharon studied more, cultivated different friends, especially others interested in photography, and searched for new hobbies. Ox had run away by this time, to no one's surprise, especially his family's. Phantom had been jailed for breaking probation. Max Gallardi sighed and said good riddance, while Sharon thrived with Felicia's (it had been Michele's) Minolta on her shoulder. In jeans, sneakers, and checkered shirt, she carried the camera like a shield. Scorched on the casing and straps, but with a new lens, the camera became a powerful defense, and weapon, in her war with the outside world.

She graduated that June, entered the communications program at college, and, after four years of virtually faultless behavior, took a job on *The Weekly Times*. This was another "achievement," for Felicia as well as the paper, and the mayor, smiling with that accomplishment, urged Felicia's promotion on the force: *Sergeant* Potenza, he chortled to reporters, as if the words had magic in them.

Stories about Felicia filled newspapers throughout the state, and when she, along with Max's help, stopped a van heading into town with a stash of cocaine coming in from the Caribbean, Felicia's picture, a close up taken by Sharon, appeared on the cover of the state magazine: "Men provide strength, women give the police humanity."

She and Sharon took an apartment and furnished it, fumbling into bed together in laughter and relief the afternoon they carried an antique mahogany dresser up the steps only to find it wouldn't fit through either of their bedroom doors. Sharon, tender, soft, yet surprisingly aggressive as they kissed, never seemed to quiet her energy, even when they crawled under the covers for sleep. Later, leaving the bedroom in the dark, they stared at the dresser and laughed, regarding its bulky Empire shape as a policeman guarding the bathroom door. They tried again, turning the dresser sideways, on end, toward the bias, and even upside down, only to find that nothing eased it through the jambs. Removing the bedroom doors made no difference. Finally they let the dresser squat in the middle of the hallway, alone. It blocked the entrance to both their rooms;

they had to work around it on the way to the shower or into each other's bed. Still, as Sharon said, they could share it (and each other) daily, when they looked for clothes in the morning, and that lessened the inconvenience. At the same time the light from a small stain glass window at the end of the hall lent the dark mahogany a charming burnished color in the dawn.

❖

At first, Felicia couldn't imagine a happier life, although she dreamed about Michele (and Ox) almost nightly and found, to her disappointment, that time with Sharon had more business moments in it than funny, intimate hours. In fact, Sharon's surprising energy extended outside the bedroom to many other people. She planned frequent, crowded parties, cooking and serving herself. Once her job took hold, she also planned photographic excursions — work mostly, occasionally for fun — but always with other photographers and hikers, rarely Felicia. She hiked mountain ranges in New England, Canada, and the Rockies. During fall and spring, she passed hundreds of weekend hours at wilderness survival courses in Montana and Idaho, then in the newspaper darkroom developed photographs of trees and wilderness scenes. She sent her photographs to magazines and newspapers throughout the country and a few saw print. She won a prize in a state contest for one and another in an American folklife competition. A third hung in a national conservation exhibit touring the eastern seaboard.

Alone despite her seemed happiness, Felicia found herself during breakfast or dinner staring out windows across enormous passes of empty silence. For two winter months, she affected busyness to cover her free afternoons and evenings. Sharon organized fieldtrips with new friends, attended more photography and wilderness courses until, eventually, Felicia saw it as a permanent pattern.

"Photography is my life," Sharon shouted one morning during an argument near the mahogany dresser. "It has nothing to do with you or us. I can't give you more of my time. That's all. Not now."

"But I —"

"Fil, I can't do it. I won't."

"Sharon, I don't want to be a pain. But we were happy. You made us happy. I thought we —"

"You've made me happy too, Fil. Honestly. But with no insult intended, I have other things I want to do. I have ambitions."

"And I'm a better woman, too — because of you. Work has never done that for me."

Sharon caught her breath, blushing. Her face, normally a patchwork of pale rose and white, turned red as she shook her hair and straightened. She held a pair of pastel underpants in her hands while Felicia, shoeless, wore a police whistle on her neck and an open shirt. On the wall near the bathroom, one of Sharon's early photographs loomed above their heads: two deer, close-up, a shady grove of fern and sweetbrier blurry behind them. Felicia had always admired it, while Sharon came to dislike it and now would like to take it down.

"It's just the opposite, Fil, isn't it? — I'm the one who's supposed to be improved because of you. Ask my father, the mayor, my teachers."

Closing her eyes, Felicia turned from the dresser and buttoned her shirt. "You know what I mean. I know you're angry. But after all these years, you give me something no person, no drug, no job — or anything else — can. Or could."

"No person should," Sharon said.

❖

At times, it seems to Felicia, some fate or God is determined to say no, not only to her, but to everyone around her, except a certain happy few. She knew she still loved Michele, a brilliant, beautiful source of pain that would not disappear, and ever practical, she came to view Sharon as a less than perfect, necessary replacement. Sharon could not offer the gorgeous color of life that Michele managed simply by existing. But her grit and strength, her involvement with ideas so tied to light and form they were somehow permanent, earned Sharon her right to a special place in Felicia's life. And, of course, Sharon had survived darkness, too — her mother's death, days of grunge with Ox, the struggle for independence from her father until an angel, dressed in blue and obviously needy herself, arrived in a Saxton cruiser. Proud of this real human achievement in her career, Felicia felt humbled by it too, regarding her desire for Sharon as simple but privileged, intense yet somehow undeserved.

"You must be disappointed," she said, a few weeks after their argument before the dresser. "Life hasn't treated you as well — or as fairly — as you want."

At the sink in their kitchen this time, Sharon threw down the rubber dish-sponge and shook her head. Felicia sat at the table. She had just come home after graveyard patrol, ready to tell Sharon over breakfast that she was about to sign a lease on her own apartment. But Sharon prepared for a trip herself that morning and did not have much time. She had already eaten. Wearing jeans, hunting boots, and a green flannel shirt that stretched smoothly across her neck and shoulders, she offered Felicia a cup of coffee but refused to look in her eyes as she described an assignment she had taken in the western mountains of the state.

"For two weeks," she said, adjusting her apron, "a nature shoot. Bears, white-tale deer, whatever."

But with all the excitement, an edge of sadness cut through Sharon's voice. Felicia listened, sensing something more than news of the assignment.

"You're having a bad day already?" she asked, peeved and maybe a little tired.

Rinsing a plate layered with a chevron of suds, Sharon placed it in the drainer and nodded. Then she turned, suddenly crying and red-faced.

"Oh, fuck it, Fil, let's not fight this morning. You know with us it's not just a matter of bad days anymore."

"Bad months? What is it then — me?"

Sharon stared at the floor.

Felicia crossed the room and, in front of Sharon, waited. "Nothing so important as you," Sharon said. She looked at Felicia's badge, touched it, and like a sister, embraced Felicia with wet, soapy arms. In the morning light Felicia saw fresh tears run down Sharon's cheeks and, surprised, reached for a tissue from the box on the table.

"Do you have something to tell me?"

Sharon nodded.

Felicia half-guessed the worst. "Are you afraid I won't sympathize or understand?"

"Don't be silly. God! — It has nothing to do with sympathy."

"I'm not young, but I'm also not stupid. I can understand."

Sharon laughed, finger to her lips as she lay the tissue down. "Fil, I never said you were stupid. Or old. Things have just changed for both of us. It's time to realize that."

"I do," Felicia said. But then she felt something — a mood, a shadow — and, realizing that her wrists trembled, she joined her hands before her eyes. How do you say the impossible? She looked at Sharon but could not bring herself to mention her apartment.

"Fil, you're wonderful. You've always been wonderful. But that's the problem: I can't possibly give you everything you deserve."

"Who asked for everything?"

"Where are *you* going?" Sharon said. "What will help

you get there?"

Felicia grinned, not at the questions, but at all the possible answers she might give. At that time, she thought of Michele as a child ripped from her womb, handed to another, quickly growing out of reach. And touch. Angrily, she shouted, as if something else were lost with the child, "Where am I going? — Where have I been for all this time? Here in Saxton. With, and without, you."

Sharon picked up a platter and, while rinsing, fumbled it, dropping it on the floor. She sobbed, remaining at the sink while Felicia regarded the pale, dripping soap on the shards of the stoneware and then Sharon's paler, suds-covered hands. She groaned, clenching her fists. Just a few months ago they laughed at such incidents: Dressers in the middle of hallways; soap and broken dishes on the floor; love in the air; stain glass colors on dark wood.

"Fil, I don't know what else we can say."

"It's late. This is not doing either of us much good."

Sharon's face flushed and her mouth closed. She, too, fought back something awful. Wiping her eyes, she drained the sink while Felicia threw out the broken platter and wiped the floor.

After packing a few things upstairs, Sharon entered the kitchen again, paused for Felicia's kiss, hesitant and sisterly now. As Felicia stood on the porch and watched her friend throw gear and backpack into the car, its blasting radio supporting a brave, soldierly smile and sisterly wave, she began to comprehend, or hoped she did.

In some dumb men's magazine lying around the station (near a photograph of a naked redhead milking a cow: words underlined by Max and presented to Felicia as a joke), she had read that "even the simplest women speak in a wide variety of languages." Felicia nodded as she remembered her fury when she told Max what to do with that magazine. Yet now she knew that she had never learned to decipher another person's intimate language — Michele's, Sharon's, and, amazingly, not even her own. You turn your back on people. You hike your own steep trail from day to day. Enough is enough.

Retreating to the bedroom, Felicia paused at the dresser and found a fresh red rose with a handwritten note. For a moment, but only one, she thought it might mean something. It brought back the trembling to her wrists and a surge of angry helplessness at the rumbling earth and sky. "I can not return," Sharon wrote. "When I get back, I'm leaving the apartment for good. I'll never forget what we have meant to each other."

Felicia burned the note, leaving the cinders in an empty ashtray on the dresser. "Keep everything yourself," she scribbled on her own small scrap of paper. "Nothing can be more simple."

She gathered a few things, packing books, clothes, and some personal items. She dropped the key into the ashtray, moved the dresser against her bedroom doorway, and, with the rose now jutting from the clip on her holster, carried everything out of the apartment before breakfast.

A MAN OF HIS TIME

"**T**his is not a war," he told everybody before leaving, "it's a... a... simply a transition." And here he is once again — Roger Larusso — crossing a bridge, preparing to pass through the doors of a new time zone: another world, maybe, but more striking than that, as he thinks of it, into another tense.

Still he feels the pull of familiar landmarks. Streamlined modern-looking buildings, bright stripes and multi-colored paint peeling, more industrial plants and factories. And still the same ragout stew of traffic: drivers, cigarettes stuck to their pouting lower lips, striving to get somewhere, anywhere, before somebody, anybody, else. Carbon-covered, pock-marked houses of stone and cement lining the rail tracks and, as they ride in closer to the city, the same explicit adver-tisements — feet, thighs, buttocks, and boobs — selling shoes, soda pop, and cabbage casseroles. Buildings loom, as if lost in the smog of a time warp, higher, grander on the approach to the circular road and the ancient gate into the city. He feels nostalgia mixed with the dread of a country boy coming home.

Roger doesn't recognize anything specific yet — he lived south, in a humbler neighborhood, in the 1970s — but as soon as the driver passes the railroad station and begins to work his way down the grand boulevard, side streets, cafes, even pedestrians, take on familiar looks and shapes. The cab jerks to a halt at a hotel just around the corner from the new industrial tower. Roger pays the fare, enters, salutes the *patron,* an old acquaintance, and takes a cup of his fresh coffee while the room is prepared. Finally, he retreats to the telephone booth behind the breakfast room to call Katharina.

"Yes, who is this? —" Her son answers, voice cracked and strained yet surprisingly mature. It has been ten years since Roger last saw the boy.

"Jean?"

"Yes..."

"Is your mother —" After a pause, he adds, "I'd like to talk to Katharina Mouiller."

"Madame Mouiller is busy at this time. Please, who is this?"

He hears impatience in Jean's voice, not unusual considering the circumstances, but the edge is enough to make him hesitate about his name. "An old friend," he says at last, "of your father. Roger Larusso."

Jean says nothing. For a few painful seconds Roger wonders if the boy has forgotten him, or, worse, hung up. Then he hears him breathe and in an attempt to break through to a former time says he is sorry about his father's sudden death. Jean thanks him, not warmly, promising he will "inform" his mother that Roger called. He takes the number and address of the hotel and says Katharina will call back as soon as she is free.

"You must understand," Jean adds, as if it were an order. "We are very busy at this time."

"I certainly do understand. If I can help in any way, just let me know."

Jean says nothing. They hang up in silence, and after a query to the hotel *patron* about funeral notices in the daily paper, Roger goes up to his room to unpack and shower. According to one paper, services for Gilbert Mouiller will take place that day in the chapel of a private school he donated money to for years; he will be buried after noon in the Mouiller family plot in the oldest cemetery of the city. Roger walks toward the boulevard, finds a cafe, drinks another coffee, and after an hour of reading papers, leaves to take a cab to the funeral.

The school is on a little side street in the university dis-

trict, between the main entrance to the university and the
eastern end of a six-lane boulevard that transverses the
city. Cars have jammed into every space on the street, with
six or seven of them parked on the sidewalk. He notices
several motorcycles, one with a sidecar, a couple of bicy-
cles, and the hearse, a nineteenth-century wagon painted
black with polished brass lamps, drawn curtains, and a
fine black horse standing before it.

The chapel is large but crowded, and as Roger slips into
an empty space on the back wall, he looks for familiar faces,
or at least ones that seem familiar. A respected Russian
writer is there, and a more famous Czech, both friends of
Gilbert; and one or two Yugoslavs who found homes with the
Mouillers on first coming to the West when the wars started.
Jean, taller but still very thin, stands near the closed casket,
his face oddly animated and smiling. He leans over a row of
chairs, speaks to a woman whom Roger takes to be
Katharina, although he can not see her clearly, and then
playfully slaps the shoulder of a boy sitting next to her: his
brother, Gustave.

A bearded, scholarly-looking man stands at a lectern to
the right of the casket, and before him, taking up two rows
of chairs just across from the Mouiller family, sits a band of
seven or eight silent, unsmiling young men, dressed in
leather jackets, with heads shaved and tattooed, or wearing
tomahawked, dyed, rainbow-colored hair. Safety pins,
straight pins, along with two or three clothespins dangle
from their ears, noses, and tongues. They move in unison,
heads turning left or right as if by signal, their pale, dark-
featured faces responding to everything gravely despite their
clownish dress. The Czech writer smiles, whispering behind
his hand to the Russian and two women between them.

The speaker begins his eulogy, his sentences clearly
enunciated, his voice expressive, though with a rough, foreign edge. He refers to Gilbert as "this good man," extolling
the gifts he gave, the lives he touched and aided, the works

begun and completed, or left unfinished. "This was our country," he says, "the best of it — safe haven for all and unmatched, generous grandeur."

Roger can not help noticing how Jean, his shoulders hunched, continues to look around and smile, curiously, foolishly, as if he were at a first communion or graduation, while mother and brother sit beside him, their heads high, intent on the speaker. Across the aisle from them, the boys, slumped forward, pins shaking as they stretch and comfort one another, maintain their silence, although occasionally a moan or a murmur rises from among them. When the speaker finishes, he nods toward the Mouillers. After a moment's hesitation Gustave rises, edging past his mother and brother. Fifteen, small-boned, dark like his father, he stands behind the lectern with his head barely visible above it. Unfolding a piece of paper, he begins to read, first uttering in a trembling voice, "My dear, dear Papa."

Tears stream down his face. His breath catches, moving the audience, the boys across from the Mouillers especially, with people sobbing and crying out from time to time as he speaks. Roger struggles for self-control, concentrating on the others around him. Gustave, noticeably trembling, struggles too — to check himself and keep a calm tone as he begins to read what is, apparently, a poem, or a poetic piece of prose. At times his voice barely rises above a whisper; at others his words emerge in a nearly full-throated shout. At the end, he lowers his head, folds the paper and puts it into his pocket. He, Jean, and four other men, teachers and administrators at the school, watch as three young students wheel the casket on its gurney toward the exit. They follow.

Now Roger sees Katharina more fully, or what he can make out of her behind a black veil. She stands beside her boys and, with her head still high, walks toward the back of the chapel. She says nothing, makes no motion of welcome, but Roger sees her glance as she passes, even though she does not nod or give a sign of recognition. Jean smiles, not for Roger but at everyone surrounding him, and looks down at a video camcorder that he carries in his hands. He adjusts the lens, and when Roger emerges through the doors to stand in the crowd on the chapel steps, he notices young Jean letting the camcorder roll while he points it: toward the building, the hearse, the casket going into the hearse, the boys in their leather jackets, tattoos, and multi-colored hairdos who are the last to file out.

The driver climbs onto the box of the hearse, looks to the sky and, with a practiced snap of his whip, starts the horse in motion.

They move slowly along the cobble-stoned streets down an ancient lane behind the university, in front of a grand monument, then across a square toward the cemetery. The streets are quiet, except for the distant hum of automobiles on the boulevard, and the only sounds they hear are the clop from the horse's hooves, the muffled shuffle of their own shoe leather against stones, and an occasional sigh or moan from a member of the party. This is one of the barest, most private quarters in the city, and its effect on the mourners this day is shattering. Roger watches Katharina and her boys behind the cart, marveling at her sense of presence, her show of bravery, especially since Gustave seems to have a hard time remaining erect, and Jean, though not taping now, still carries the camcorder in his hands.

They enter the cemetery from an entrance near the farmers' market and, crossing in front of civil guards who stand saluting, they walk to the west side of the grounds and bury Gilbert not fifty steps from the grave of a famous poet and his hated stepfather, whose spirits, Gilbert used to tell Roger, will glare at each other and shake their fists to entertain him for eternity. With the steady hum of traffic from the nearby market street, it is impossible to hear the words of the man who eulogizes over the grave. But when Katharina and Jean drop roses on the coffin and

Gustave, sobbing, follows with a copy of the words he has read in the chapel, the collective sighs of everyone, especially the young men in leather jackets and pins, seem to drown out everything else. Katharina takes her boys by the shoulders and draws them close before lowering her arms and, hands clasped, walking through the cemetery gate without waiting for anyone else.

Her head remains high, Roger notices. He is not sure how much of that is pose since, when he finally catches up with her on the old street, she is looking down at her feet, not responding to anything around her.

"Kat... Katharina," he calls just above a whisper. After two more attempts, he sees her stop and, just beneath the veil, smile.

"Roger Larusso. So nice to see you. Jean said you had called."

"I'm sorry about Gilbert," he mutters. Then, awkwardly, "It was quite a blow."

She nods. Through the veil Roger sees her hazel eyes still dry, her complexion still ruddy, the glow on her left cheek just hidden under her hair. She turns to continue up the cobble-stoned street, and he falls into step beside her, matching her steady gait ("feet on the ground," she used to say, "Gilbert is all in ether"), her square-shouldered, Slavic acceptance of life marking her pace as well as her posture.

"You are taking it well. How did it happen?"

She smiles, folding her hands, palms touching, fingers straight out as if she were praying. "Ah, you don't read the papers, Roger. You never missed before. It's your profession."

"Kat — ?"

She waves. "He died in an accident — a bomb, placed in a trash container near the Metro. It went off as we walked by."

"Christ, I'm sorry. I read about some bombing, but I didn't know he ... And you were with him? How — ?"

She shakes her head. "It barely touched us. He lunged

into the street to protect me and was run over by a truck. A laundry truck. He died on the way to the hospital. I never saw him alive again."

She grins, oddly. Roger notices the strong resemblance to Jean.

"Another horrible political bombing! What a waste!"

Katharina shrugs. "Who knows? Our times."

Roger says nothing, shakes his head. They walk up the street, aware of others catching up, then passing by. They remain silent, Katharina occasionally greeting or being greeted by others in a more or less formal manner. Back at the school, she stands inside the doors to the chapel and, without lifting her veil, receives people in front of a stand of lilies and a table of light refreshments set in the vestibule. Roger leaves her there when Jean and Gustave enter, retreating to a corner to sit and balance a cup of coffee on his knee. Gustave stands near his mother, dark suit, white shirt and grave manner creating the appearance of a little Gilbert. Jean, with his tie loosened now, walks around the room with the camcorder at his shoulder filming everything.

The Czech and the Russian smile and turn away as he approaches them. The boys in leather, metal, and wood whisper as they pass in front of the camcorder. Then, with their hands splayed and twitching hungrily, they arrange themselves at a table and gather platefuls of little sandwiches that they bring into the corner near Roger. Loud, clumsy, unbelievably crude, they sit along the wall, talking to each other and to bystanders while their ugly, blue-headed leader, his face pitted with acne scars and pimples, attempts a conversation with Roger.

"Not bad for Gilbert," he says, appraising the surroundings. "How did you know him?"

"Work. And through some of his political" — Roger searches for the word in the young man's language —"Conferences." Finally, he adds, emphasizing the English, "Meetings."

"Ah, you are British!"

"American," Roger says.

The skinhead nods, smiling, looking Roger over as if he knows everything now. Sticking out his tongue (with a green rhinestone in it) he adds, "Gilbert loved you Americans — *loved* you — the old bastard."

He begins to talk about popular music — Madonna, Michael Jackson, Bon Jovi, Guns 'n' Roses, Pearl Jam. Roger tries to respond knowledgeably, but the boy quickly senses that none of those artists make this American's kind of sound.

"You like Elvis," he says at last, appraising Roger's age. "Gilbert adored Elvis. And Tony Bennett."

Roger laughs. "Gilbert's taste was more eclectic than mine. I stopped liking Elvis when I — When I left back there the first time. And I hardly listen to Tony Bennett — or even Sinatra."

"Dylan! You like Dylan! I know it!"

The young man smiles, swallowing half a sandwich with a gape-toothed grin. The rhinestone flashes in and out of bread crust, cheese, and meat. He turns and murmurs to his friends, his words fast, his flushed, melon-like head blocking his lips so Roger cannot understand. Whatever the boy says, his friends stare at Roger, their mouths wide, their tongues an accumulated showcase of cheap stones and metal. Still, to them, he has done some odd, even shameful, thing.

"I don't like popular music at all," he announces, a boy again, somehow, lost in a foreign land. "I like serious music: Bach, Beethoven — Stravinsky."

"Pah! — What are you, snob?"

The leader with the tattooed head grins and pops another sandwich, whole, into his mouth. When a second boy with pink, green, and orange feathers woven through his crewcut hair leans in his direction, Roger raises his hand.

"Gilbert taught me the classics, you know. Through him I learned to like them all. He played them on the piano for me. As illustration."

"What — Gilbert, playing? Since when —"

Roger nods — truly snobbish, he hopes. "He had many talents, and he loved to play good music, especially modern."

"What? That old ... Gilbert? He never —"

They lean forward in disbelief. The seven of them (Roger counts now that they surround him so closely) stare almost as if they are angry. "He liked all kinds of music," Roger says. "That was one of his charms. He liked jazz, classical, rock'n'roll. He was that way with everything — open."

The leader, a tear breaking loose now, clenches his fist and shakes it. An engorged penis, tattooed in red and black, shimmers across his knuckles. "That was a man," he says. "A real ... We'll never see another like him!"

His friends raise their fists and shout in unison: "*Gilbert!*"

Roger smiles but, embarrassed now that people are obviously staring at them, decides to leave his seat. He looks across the room, pretending to see someone he needs to talk with. Rising, he notices Jean pointing the camcorder toward them, and as he makes his way back toward the table of flowers, he covers his face. Jean tracks him from the tattooed head and the boy with the feathers until he reaches Katharina.

"Please, put that away! Show some respect for your poor, dear father," Roger says, firmly.

Jean grimaces, letting the camcorder drop to his side like a weapon he wants to hide — or keep ready. But then he grins, blushing foolishly, and, looking at the crowd surrounding them, nods as if he has made a significant point. "Jean, please," Katharina says. "Mr. Larusso is right. This is not a celebration. Put the camera away."

He raises it, pointing the lens at Katharina and Roger and letting the tape role. "*Maman,*" he says. "Smile. Show us how pretty you are."

"No, no," Gustave says, raising his hand to cover the lens. "Don't be cruel, Jean. Be nice — for Papa's sake."

Jean pulls the camcorder back, aims it for a moment at his brother, and then, silent, stalks away. Gustave blushes, lowering his head. Katharina looks at Roger, sighing. "He will not accept it," she says. "He is stubborn. He will not see that things have changed."

Gustave arrives with another cup of coffee, kisses her veiled cheek, and walks off to find his brother. An uneasy moment passes while Katharina shifts on her feet and, sighing, sips her coffee. She wants to talk, Roger is sure, yet she also wants to be correct with the rest of the guests, some of whom, a group of Croats and Poles, stop to pay their respects before leaving, others of whom simply hope to learn more about Gilbert's final moments or discuss Katharina's future plans. Gilbert's brother, Henri, fat, amiably crude, one glass eye impervious to the smoke curling from a cigarette between his swollen, bleeding lips, clutches her elbow from behind and turns her toward a group of three elderly men — gray, short, bearing unmistakably the stamp of the Mouiller family frame — comical despite their mourning clothes.

"Our cousins," Henri says, "Michel, Richard, Bertrand. I believe you have never met them."

They bow, bumping into themselves, their toes clownishly catching under one another's heels. They have always avoided Gilbert, Roger knows, but Katharina, oblivious, shakes each of their hands and says — a lie, he is sure — that Gilbert spoke of them often. After she introduces them to Roger, they bow, expressing condolences and, with Henri, wander off to find Gustave and Jean.

Katharina barely gets out: "Oh, he is impossible! Did you smell?" Roger nods, still sniffing the mixture of sweat, tobacco, and must that fades as Henri waddles away. "I can't stand to be near him," she says, "much less touched."

Katharina brushes the sleeve of her dress and looks at the floor in disgust.

"He's trying to do the right thing, as a brother. And as

an uncle. It's all he can do."

She laughs. "He doesn't know the right thing. He doesn't care. Gilbert always said Henri was selfish, and he's proved it hundreds of times. The cousins, too."

"Well..."

She nods, lowering her voice. "I shouldn't expect any-thing better. Gilbert was different. You know; he grew."

Roger looks away. "Best not to worry about those things now," he tells her.

Her head sinks. He can almost see her lose color beneath the veil. Her chin trembles. "Oh, *Ruggero mio,* I don't know what to do. I feel... I feel so..."

She stops. Her head shakes as she stares at his feet. Self-consciously, he takes her arm and leads her to a chair in the corner behind the flowers. Katharina has not sat since leaving the chapel, and now her body sinks wearily into the chair. Roger freshens her cup with some coffee, and then sits beside her. He tries to get her to remove her hat, at least to lift the veil above her eyes. She refuses; she wants to do the right thing by Gilbert, she says, and that means retaining the widow's appearance.

"He was so sad," she says, "so small when they put him into the ambulance."

She straightens her back, sips her coffee, and again stands to talk to people surrounding the table. Henri returns with the three cousins, and soon Gustave and Jean arrive, Jean noticeably without his camcorder. The seven talk together, with guests, most of whom seem to know Henri rather than Katharina, occasionally breaking into their conversation. Even the young men in leather and pic-tures stop to talk for a few minutes while making a slow, boisterous exit, passing in front of Roger and raising their fists as they leave.

"Take care, American! Remember Elvis!"

People look from them to him and laugh. He blushes, turning away in anger and saying nothing. His shame persists, and soon he begins to grow restless among the crowd around Katharina. Finally, Roger taps her on the shoulder, excusing himself by saying he has some business across the city. But as he leaves the chapel, turning toward the cathedral steeples for a nostalgic walk along the banks of the river, he hears a voice and turns to see Katharina, on the steps, running toward him.

"Here," she says, "I want to give you this."

She hands him an envelope with a photograph in it. He opens it and sees Gilbert: Smiling, his glasses glinting above his thick, dark lips, he pushes back a wisp of thinning hair. Behind him, on motorcycles, sit the seven young men in leather and, among them, Katharina, and another man, an American, Carl Becker, whose grim smile makes him look like an unwilling participant.

"Gilbert and his brats," Katharina says, not smiling. "His two favorites among them."

Roger looks away.

"And did you know Carl Becker is ill?"

He nods. "I heard as I was leaving. I'll visit him just before I cross into Sarajevo and beyond."

"That disease. Everyone's susceptible now."

She takes Roger's hand and stops. When a motorcycle engine begins to roar, she pulls him into a little courtyard beside the chapel. In a corner, behind the statue of a bearded, long-robed prelate, she puts her hand on his shoulder, lifts her veil, and kisses him, passionately, on the mouth.

"Is it still there," she asks, at last, "still — ?"

"What?"

"Don't play with me, *Ruggero mio.* You know." Katharina takes off her hat and, pulling aside a thick portion of her chestnut hair, thrusts her right cheek toward him. A large, liver-colored spot, a birthmark shaped something like a ginkgo leaf, splays from her ear along her cheek and jawbones, almost to her lips. He draws his breath.

"Is it — God's tattoo, as Gilbert called it?"

He says nothing. Beyond the wall, the roar of four, five, then six motorcycles booms off the buildings, rattles windows, shakes the bearded prelate standing to their left. Through the courtyard gate, Roger sees Jean, camcorder at his shoulder again, taping his father's brats as they, circling from somewhere beyond the chapel, lower their heads and speed down the street.

"Is it? Don't play with me, Roger. Is the mark still there?" She nudges him.

"You know it is, Katharina."

"Then you don't love me," she tells him, replacing her hat and pulling down her veil.

Mysterious again, she hesitates before walking through the gate.

"Kat — Katharina, we..."

She waves, turning back toward the chapel as Roger searches for words. "God wills it," she calls, smiling. "I came to this country with clothes on my back and this on my face. Nothing else. Gilbert loved me. Now I will be buried here with him — and it, too."

He clutches the photograph, silent, staring after her. He lowers his hands as Jean, crying out and stepping around the cement column of the statue, approaches. The camcorder at his shoulder, whirring.

AMERICA

MACHO MAUDIT
(For Alex)

"The poorhouse or the children," my father always said. Frustrated, avoiding yet another dead end job in his middle years, my father, following an Italian's *via vecchia*, counted on me to add to his meager part time income. What is more he expected me, the older son, now the last child home since my brother, Sal, had begun his search for the perfect wave at a very early age, to live with and support him and my mother until they died. At twelve, I welcomed the idea. At nineteen, it all struck me as old-fashioned.

"Dad, suppose I don't want to live where you live? Suppose I want to move to California, with Sal? Or to Europe?"

He'd look at me in disbelief, a waved hand or frown doggedly dismissing future escapes. "What do you want to do that for? — You're going to teach. You can live with us. Look at all the money you'll save."

"Suppose I want to get married, like Cora?"

He'd look at me as if that weren't on the chart yet, but he had a way of ignoring it as well. We were living in a two family house outside Philly when this part of the dialogue started, and he'd say my wife and I could take the apartment on the second floor. We'd live rent-free, and my family and I could save for a house of our own. It was an argument that, with its stubborn blue-collar logic, always put me at a loss. I had begun to think of myself as a song writer, a poet, of all things, and I could never think of saving for anything, much less a house and a family. I needed independence and experience, but when I said that to my father one day he looked at me as if I were thinking about dating goats.

My mother, once harboring visions of performing in opera, called it an impossible dream. People worked, put money away, lived, if they were lucky, off their accumulations in old age. Yet her fatigued, defeated eyes always preserved a ray of hope for me: we came this far; my child actually might break through. So while my father insisted on it daily, she merely hoped that I conform, even when things changed rather quickly in the early sixties and we moved to a smaller, cheaper, one-family house closer to downtown.

"We can expand the attic into a second floor apartment," my father told me, as we carried boxes through the front door one Saturday afternoon. "For me and your mother. At our age, we won't need very much."

"A logical, self-sacrificing conclusion," I muttered as we dropped boxes onto the living room floor.

He looked from me to my mother near the kitchen door and smiled sheepishly. Our move occurred late in the fall of my freshman year in college, after I had decided to live my own life, a more authentic one, I thought, even if it was in an attic of some foreign city. Or in a cabin in the woods, like my rustic hero, Thoreau.

I won't make a big deal of it; nothing dramatic happened. I went to northern Jersey for two nights and days with a friend and an acquaintance of his. One Friday afternoon soon after the move we packed sleeping bags, cooking utensils, a knapsack of clothes, and a couple flashlights into a car, crossed the state line, and headed north for the distant New Jersey woods. We left the highway, drove through the hills of Sussex County, and by a series of back roads and tractor trails, came to a farm called (the name was continental, Italian even, shocking so far from Philadelphia) "Blazi's Glen."

The swarthy owner, with huge arms, a long nose, and minimalist, dark-haired crew-cut, allowed campers to stay on his property for the weekend, if they promised not to fish the stream or hunt the surrounding woods. No problem. No weapons or rods lay in the trunk or back seat, so Mr. Cosimo Blazi, taking a five-dollar bill from each of us, just waved us toward an opening in some trees and said we could camp anywhere we wanted. We parked beneath the trees, took the equipment from the car, and in one trip carried everything down the glen to the pool of a waterfalls, where we set up our camp.

We put up a lean-to instead of a tent — the three of us intending to sleep under the stars — and laid out sleeping bags and cooking gear before we gathered wood for the fire. We placed the food in canvas bags, tying them to a bush on the bank before dumping the bags into the pool. Then we swam, hiked, and started a fire. By the time the sun set, we had eaten dinner and were toasting marshmallows; by the time we ate them we fell silent and rested on our sleeping bags. I had never slept outdoors before, yet aside from dim fears of a bear or wolf, I felt surprisingly at ease. The falls shushed and, because we were sheltered from the wind, practically nothing else moved or made a sound. It was not a large falls, raising a pleasant murmur rather than a roar, quieting, rather than drowning out, the sound of the fire, or the buzz of the occasional insect. I looked up to study the flicker of the campfire on the branches overhead, peering through their shadows to some faint white specks in the sky behind them. I also looked across the fire to one of my companions reading a book. With the turpentine lamp on, the water beside him, and the darkness beyond, he seemed like a figure in a woodcut. An ax jutted from the tree at his shoulder. He smoked a corncob pipe, and to a city-suburban boy who had never seen these things before, it was — what else? — magical. It walked me through the looking glass world of Independence Hall and the Liberty Bell into the rougher, combative one of Davy Crockett and Wyatt Earp, both of whom, even more than Ben Franklin, still had the power of myth for me. I saw the ax as a practical weapon against the elements and threatening animals; I could see the book in my friend's lap as something meaningful to a man living outdoors: the comfort of print, the lively presence of another human mind.

Next morning I rose earlier than the other two. I washed my face in a cold stream for the first time, then, on a whim, followed the water as it overflowed the pool and moved deeper into the woods. Dawn, just after; the bright blue sky glowing above, the light beneath the branches of the trees still a little dim. As I ambled along the stream, I passed through some bushes and came to another, shallower falls. A gray, rock wall went up on my right, a sloping hill of earth and brush rose on my left. The water settled in a pool for a moment, then, after a pause, rushed over the edge and fell onto several boulders below. I stopped, moved by the sound of the water, as well as the sight of trees and sky. For a moment I felt like flying, or leaping, somehow expressing the lightness I felt among all this natural weight. It loomed — huge, strong — with no conscience to care. If I jumped, I would fall onto the water and rock below. If I stepped into the stream, it would sweep me over. I would shatter, be hurt or killed, but not because I had done something sinful or illegal. It would be a simple, *natural* phenomenon that I might fight as I went down — because of my instinct for survival — but water and stone would do their mutual work and trees would continue reaching for the light.

Dizzy, I pulled myself away from the water, and after climbing down to the lower pool, returned to camp. My friends and I cooked breakfast, the best I've ever eaten, and spent the day swimming, reading, and hiking for firewood. It rained for a short period that afternoon, the three of us huddling under the lean-to while we talked. Before sleep that night, I opened a book of Walt Whitman's poems and read in it. *Leaves of Grass*, the title, never meant so much.

"Did you like it?" my friend asked, after we hiked our gear up the glen next morning and began the drive back home. He knew I had never camped before. He had frankly wondered if I, born and raised on a street of 50 by 75 foot lots, would be disappointed. He had also wondered if I would get along with our companion, an expert woodsman from New England.

"I loved it," I said, grinning. "I don't feel like going back." He laughed, punching my arm.

"Honest?"

"Honest."

He howled, pounding my back. "Hey, you Guinea slicker. I finally made a man out of you. I finally made you take a shit in the woods."

He was not quite so gleeful when I got out of the car at home a couple of hours later. My parents sat in the macadam driveway with some neighbors and Sal, home for a visit, with a duffel bag of dirty laundry at his feet. A metal fence spread behind them, and beyond it were the cement backs of a small church and a store with a huge parking lot between. I sighed as my friends' car left the driveway and rolled away. "How did it go?" my mother said, as I walked toward her, knapsack in my hand. She had on a house dress, sleeveless, with ruffled straps on the shoulders. For the warmer weather, she wore her hair cut short.

"I really had a good time," I said, smiling. "I think I'm going again."

My father put down a newspaper and stared at me. Except for occasional trips to the park to look at blossoming cherry trees, he had never taken me, Sal, or Cora for walks in the woods. But he nodded and smiled, as if he could understand.

"Don't you wish you had been a Boy Scout?" my mother asked. "This could have been a regular thing."

I shook my head. Men in our neighborhood saw Boy Scouts as prissy at best: "What do they do in the woods without women?" they asked.

"A Boy Scout? Oh, I don't know," I said, covering a laugh. "Maybe I will be. Maybe there's still time."

Maybe there was. I never — except for sporadic trips to my sister's house — had left home before, not even for a day. I never, really, had been outside the comfort (and dis-comfort) of family life. I went into the house, up to my room and without unpacking, wrote a poem about the weekend. It was about sleeping among trees, perceiving time with a glimpse of sky through the branches overhead; it was about feeling helpless while sliding down the side of a waterfall. I finished the poem within an hour, then half-spoke, half-chanted it into a tape recorder. Lines had never come so easily. After I read them and replayed the tape for myself, I took out the information I had received from a university writing program the previous winter. Money did-n't seem an obstacle that night. Nor did a move from home, beyond the Mississippi. Hearing the sound of water hum-ming over distant rocks, I read the information and decid-ed to apply.

Photographs from the family album plainly reveal the changes in me between the ages of seventeen and twenty-one. There is one picture of me, taken during the summer after my junior year in high school, that I just recently pulled from my wallet and pasted on an album page. I am in a baseball uniform, standing on the pitcher's mound, staring into home plate for the catcher's signal. "St. Agatha's C.Y.O.", is scrawled across my chest, and the cap above my glasses has an interwoven S and A. I smile, big front teeth glistening, grin pushing the flab of my soft cheeks into a squint around my eyes. When I look at the picture today, I still cannot believe who I am. The bulk of the uniform adds to the bulk of my body. It is hard to know I could lift a leg high enough to throw a ball.

"That's me," I used to say, in my father's voice when he displayed the wounds on his head and feet from encoun-ters with a door, a garden tool, or some other unspecified object. "Two hundred and forty pounds; size forty-four waist on the trousers. By the end of the summer I was down to a thirty-six."

I loved to tell people that, especially years later, as a soldier.

I could throw and catch pretty well, when I got to the ball. I could hit too, but I held the world's record for slowness on the base paths. By the time I was seventeen, I understood that beautiful girls in our neighborhood preferred faster, leaner boys who did not read as much as I did, and I began to diet accordingly, cutting down on books and food. I lost sixty pounds in a little more than two months, shrank the size of my baseball trousers five times, and caused daily arguments with my parents about my health and school work.

"You need a little calcium," my mother would say, her hand flourishing a knife full of butter to encourage me.

"I don't want any, Ma. Just leave me alone."

I would pull a plate of steamed vegetables away as she tried to dump some cheese sauce on them, and then open up a body-building magazine. Quads, triceps, lats. I wanted them all, in the highest definition, but my parents had other ways of measuring fitness.

"What about cereals and grains? You've got to have protein. Your brain has to grow. Your body will take care of itself. What is your mind going to thrive on?"

"The fat of my belly. It's quite apparent I've stored enough to think on for years."

We went on like that throughout the summer. Meanwhile my father and I argued over trousers sizes that he, a tailor, was expected to adjust downward weekly in order to avoid any Chaplinesque bagginess in the rear. I worked at a downtown men's store near Temple, played my usual amount of baseball and softball, did sit-ups and push-ups as much as two hundred and fifty times a day and, instead of the library, visited the local YMCA nightly to work with weights. It was a pleasure when, toward the end of August, I put on my first tight-fitting polo shirt, and it was even greater when I bought my first pair of pegged and pleated pants. Levis, cotton, not the wool trousers my father usually made for me. His style was too tailored, too genteel. Moving into Philly after my junior year in high school, we lived in an exclusively Italian neighborhood for the first time in my life. It changed my style of dress. No more tasteful, conservative suits draping my overly jellied frame; I wanted snug pegged pants, pink and black dress shirts tight around the waist, blossoming in the shoulders and biceps, pointy black shoes we called "fly-weights," sideburns and a greasy 1950s curl drooping over my forehead. In our previous, suburban neighborhoods, I had worn a sedate crew-cut, loose-fitting beige slacks and plaid button-down sport shirts. We spanned a gap of years and culture when we moved to that new street, and the focus of the shift lay in my body and clothes. No more Mr. Plump and Personable.

The shift took final form during the summer of my trip to the Jersey woods. Photographs show it all: the longer hair, the leaner shirts, the sideburns gradually creeping below my earlobes. There is a picture of me sitting on the mailbox in front of a grocery store, where my friends and I smoked and talked through most of our summer nights. It still makes me stare: Lock of hair curling down my forehead, sleeves of my polo shirt rolled above moderately bulging biceps, trousers flaring at hips and knees while narrow cuffs hug my exposed ankles. I wear thin white socks that peek, like signs along the turnpike, between the trouser cuffs and, of course, my new black flyweights. My head rolls back, a pose of punkish nobility. And a new prop, a cigarette, dangles from my lips. I smile pleasantly, but my fist is cocked like a pistol beneath my resting chin.

"Why do you want to look like a dago?" my mother said whenever she saw me staring at that picture. "Why don't you stay home with us more often? More important, why don't you do your schoolwork anymore? And, please, let your father make you decent clothes."

"Come on, Ma! He doesn't have any sense of style."

"Dago style, you mean. You think dressing like that and standing on the corner makes you attractive? It won't get you anywhere. Let your father..."

"He makes me look like an old man!" — which, with intentional nastiness, clearly meant he made me look like him.

My mother expanded the argument with a dire prediction of my awful future: no doctoring or lawyering, not even writing or teaching. Just an Italian-American roustabout, or hood — "One of them!" she'd say, with a toss of her head.

Although we never used the M-word, I occasionally did emulate tough guy characters or workers, at least outwardly, especially in view of the young men ("Kings on peasants' errands," according to my mother) who swaggered along our neighborhood streets. In reality they aped a trendy Hollywood type: males who possess crude, soft-hearted centers. It was not lost on us that with his fortune Elvis Presley bought his parents a new house and a Cadillac; it was not lost on us that in *Rebel Without a Cause*, Jimmy Dean allows the beautiful, motherly, Natalie Wood to simmer him down; and the boldest, baddest, of them all, Brando, well, his whole career looked like a series about domesticated rebels who finally succumbed to mama. The truth showed much later, in "Last Tango," the last movie I remember seeing with my former wife, Valerie: Paul-Brando reminisces lovingly about his mother, sobs like a baby at wife Rose's bier, experiences interesting sexual tensions when he visits his mother-in-law; and finally, the young girl he has raped, washed, and subdued most brutally, plays a severe, masterly rebel herself. He dons her father's cap; she destroys him.

On our cramped block, unlike the spacious, tree-lined streets we saw and dreamed about with the help of movies or television shows, my friends and I regarded ourselves and our families as outsiders. My father, sitting next to me on the living-room couch, his sloped shoulders shaking with laughter, couldn't wear sweaters, throw a football, be an Eagle Scout, and exercise casual *laissez-faire* authority as Ozzie Nelson did. My father worked odd jobs and collected unemployment. He couldn't wear a business suit, come home to sweater and slippers, and still maintain a suave, informal respectability as did Robert Young. And while the whole neighborhood loved Desi Arnez in "I Love Lucy," we all understood that without his voice (and Lucy), his Latin name and style marked him as much an outcast as we were. In rare, touching moments of carefree innocence, my father sometimes acted like a TV dad, but he never shared two essentials: ease with money (really a laughable lack of concern) and absolute certainty that he occupied the right place in the right world while carrying his family comfortably with him.

So, I don't fool myself with that picture of me on the mailbox, as I don't fool myself with photographs from the following years: jeans, sweaters, a nylon "Zero King" jacket ("Rebel Without a Cause"), even the growing tendency to go unshaven like the Beats. It all fit some place, but I never knew clearly where. I didn't leave for college right after high school, like Sal, because I couldn't break away from home. Instead I sought a complicated independence: one foot in the faded, still enclosing family circle, other foot tapping in the dust to find a better place to rest.

Community college at first, not a distant university. Not even state teachers college, as my parents once assumed. Pictures show my confusion during those two college years because I changed daily, always returning at night to the pegged pants, flyweights, and huge-shouldered dress shirts and jackets of my youth. While attending classes, I sought respectability and strength — but with a high-toned, good-humored front. In the renovated warehouse serving as a downtown campus I laughed confidently, smiling at every camera flash. But the expression I see in yearbook photographs belies the confusion I remember feeling. I look comfortable but not with life or my particular actions in it. Men I knew at work and stood on the corner with at night spoke of college in terms of beer, orgies, and football. They imagined me chasing co-eds between stacks of books in the library or dorms where Shakespeare, physics, and Latin took second place to parties and women. They read *Playboy*, saw pictures of naked cheerleaders who were psych majors at UCLA, and assumed I slept with them regularly as I commuted day to day. I should say that Sal, in his letters from California, sometimes said he did.

These events occurred in the sixties, but my daily life was not a round of liberated sex and family security. Especially at home. My father's work went poorly. Once, after midnight, he walked through the back door severely injured, the second time in six months, with a black eye, a swollen foot, and a broken hand — from a fall, he said, while carrying stock in the back room of the men's store he sewed in. And then shortly afterward his close friend, Paolo Salvaggi — a fellow tailor — was found in his garage, doors closed and car engine running, unconscious, bruised and beaten. "Attempted suicide," the Philly newspapers said, featuring photographs of a handsome dark-haired man with a debonair waxed mustache surrounded by two congressmen, the mayor, and three international businessmen, all of whom he regularly made suits for.

My mother liked Paolo despite his flashy reputation. But she suspected something more. My father chuckled, as he had when he laughed at stories about Paolo's adventures in business and love. Now I wondered, had he, by association, been a luckier target? The look on his face said nothing, until a few mornings later the police arrived at our house. Respectful, thoughtful, they talked to both my parents for fifteen minutes in the living room. Then they asked my father to come to the station for questioning. The eyes of my mother's face and in the center of every neighbor's window along the street made all the wondering irrelevant.

❖

"Did you cooperate with them, Nick?" my mother asked.

"Yes, Sophie. But nothing happened."

"Are you accused of —"

"Nothing happened. They wanted information," my father said. "That's all."

"What were you doing in the back of the store that late at night, when you hurt yourself? I thought you were supposed to be at the Garibaldi Club. Playing cards."

"I was trying to help somebody — I told you."

"Paolo?"

He shrugged. "It had nothing to do with Paolo."

My mother nodded. My father looked pale, unsmiling. I had seen Paolo court her — as well as several of my aunts — with little smiles and gifts from local florists. There were thirty seconds or so of him in a film of my parents' 25th wedding anniversary party, where he stood near my mother, lit cheroot in hand, and kissed her on the lips. How can I describe it? The moment was gentle, proper, like a friendly touch of his hand, but something in Paolo's eyes as they parted bespoke a thousand little secrets. My father waited beside them, near the uncut anniversary cake, looking intently at the camera. He had always remained completely business-like and aloof with Paolo near my mother, as if he didn't want to notice their actions. Something about his tight lips and averted eyes in that moment, and when he returned from the police station looking so guilty, told me he had cared. I could not imagine my father doing something himself. But ... along with other angry family men? Professionals?

Whatever happened, he paid. The last we heard, Paolo

Salvaggi recovered from his wounds and went on a long voyage back to Italy where, my father told us, he began to make suits for parliamentarians and movie stars. The men's shop closed soon afterward, and my father once again had no regular work. Finally, by a variety of old contacts and "kissing ass," he said, he acquired a small newspaper shop and candy store that had stood for years, with very few customers, on a small side street a few blocks from our home. Neighborhood people sneered when they heard my father managed the store. "Numbers," one of my friends said. "Newspapers are nothing. Candy is worse. But you'll probably go to a better college — buy even better suits."

In fact we had less money to buy things with, and my father barely managed payments on the family mortgage. When in my second year a community college friend rented a cheap apartment near Temple and asked me to share it with him, I thought about it only a few seconds.

"I can't afford it. My parents won't help me."

"Neither will mine. But you can use the money you pay at home. For rent and food — your own."

"That will give them nothing to live on, or close to it. My father's not working very much."

My friend blinked. "Your brother and sister will help, won't they? You're not the only child."

"Sal?" I laughed. "And Cora?"

"Why not?"

"She has expenses of her own — a new house, children."

"Sal?"

"Surfboards. Women."

He waved his hand. I turned away. At bottom I knew that even with money I wouldn't leave my parents. Education had helped. Whitman and Thoreau also helped. But I knew that in some sense all that — including the weekend in the woods last summer — existed in a superficial world of words and ideas. For me, life was home, a rich opera of stress and doom I couldn't hear enough of. Like the characters Caruso and Mario Lanza sang, I wanted to reach upward toward a larger vision. In a conflicting impulse I also reveled in the warm lights at center stage. Posing on the mailbox fits perfectly. While I look away toward some object high in the sky (beyond the camera), my smile points forward, toward the audience, the family, and neighborly eye judging me all the time. Like the fat pitcher in a flannel uniform, my eyes gaze steadily toward home plate.

❖

"Med-ee-GAHNS!" (Americans!): Sal and I heard it many times, the crudest expression of neighborhood disdain.

Loyalty equaled family. In concentric rings followed block, working class neighborhood, *medigahn* town or city, and finally, among the women more than men, church. Having lived in a reasonably proper suburban community until high school, we were *medigahn* when our family first arrived on the streets of Philly.

Sal and I spoke politely, earned good grades, studied diligently — a fact my parents never hid — and, until the late 50s at least, wore short, nappy hair brushed straight back from our foreheads. Never an Elvis lock or hippie friz in sight. But the move changed us. By senior year we had virtually stopped studying, bragged nightly about it to our street corner friends, and so everyone considered us, me with the full scholarship to a local community college, Sal by reputation and wish on his way to something grander out West, as pulling it over on the *medigahns*. For a short while therefore, with sideburns, pegged pants, trim bodies and a pair of scholarships to higher education, the Potenza brothers were both Paysan and Medigahn.

Thus, the difficulties of our early college years: my wish to attend a Big Ten school after community college (against my father's wishes), Sal's flight to the Pacific (regardless of anybody's wishes), and my love affair with an Irish-Catholic theater student (against her mother's wishes). I would rather not write about her, but for completeness, I must. She had black hair, an ample, somewhat short-waisted body, and blue eyes (flashing, uncertain) with a personality absolutely molded to please.

"Classic," Sal used to say. "*Medigahn*, feminine version — but what does she say about you?"

We had met during the first rehearsal for a college production of the Moss Hart confection "Light Up the Sky." It is a comedy about show people performing a new play and, typical for Broadway, wrings dry all the clichés. My love played the actress Irene Livingston, flighty star of the drama, and I was simply Peter, truck-driver-turned-playwright, over-wrought author of the work.

In the beginning, Peter behaves bashfully, hesitantly, uneasy about the theatrical phonies surrounding him. Perfect for Nickie Jr., everyone said. I soon agreed. In one scene, just after the opening performance outside New York, Peter's play seems a dismal flop. His girlfriend calls long-distance to offer condolences. He wants to fold up the play, retreat to the simple, thoughtful life with her:

"Aw, honey," he whimpers over the phone, "it was lousy. The crowd laughed at the most sensitive parts. Now they want me to change it, make the ending happy, put in a bunch of happy-go-lucky goons. I'm not doing it, honey. I won't. I'm coming home — to you. ...Aw, Honey, don't ... don't cry. Please. I'm coming home ... tonight."

But after hanging up, without explanation or motivation Peter changes his mind. Brushing curls back from his forehead, he rushes into battle, his commitment to art overwhelming everything. His final lines, the last ones of the play in fact, combine the gruffness of the truck-driver-turned-playwright with the classic American bad boy and his soft-hearted need for support — distant but constant — from friends: "Alright, you stupid bastards. (*He throws his rain-coat on the chair and strides commandingly across the stage.*) Let's get to work! (*He takes out a pad, sits, begins to write. Sidney Black, the cigar-smoking producer, wears a fatherly grin.*) Act one, scene one..."

Lights fade. The company look on with happiness and relief.

It's Rocky *Predux*: Brando-Paul going the distance, Stanley Kowalski moving earth and sky again in Stella's bed.

I remember the passage vividly because I identified with Peter completely. I felt hesitant about the scene on the phone at first, but as I talked on stage I heard my voice gain volume, as if I were miked. After the one performance he saw, Sal remarked on it too. The lines seemed to come from outside myself, taking on a chesty, melodic quality, he said, though they were obviously very private. As I practiced the lines — and played them over and over during a month-long run — the speech became more a part of me each time I picked up the phone. Before long I could modulate the vowels, clip the consonants, lend them passion from the reality of my daily life. I imagined talking to my mother most of the time, although sometimes I imagined talking to Cora. But by the last performance, I said the words frequently and openly, not to one of the girls back home, but to the actress in the wings who played Irene.

❖

"You're out of there," Sal said when he met her, meaning I was ready to fold the whole life up and ride the waves, just like him.

A moment would come when I would raise my fists and glory in the spotlight, just before jumping over the footlights into the empty dark. I shoved fellow students around the aisles of the library once or twice, hung up the phone whenever Irene mentioned dating someone else, walked out in a huff after a frustrating hour or two with her in my friend's apartment (the one I should have shared), and stood screaming obscenities at the top of my lungs in front of her house, her mother's man-in-the-moon eyes evident behind the living room curtains. Edgy, I took a bus to the local police club with a friend and shot .22 caliber bullets at cardboard men in masks for hours. Then I carried my fury home and argued with my parents, blaming them for my messy life's stagnation, the romantic and vocational voids before me. Some truck-driver-turned-playwright: Sinatra, eighty and searching for Nancy with a laughing face; Presley, fat, sloppy, finished at forty; and the coolest of them all, Joe Di, sending flowers to Marilyn's grave after all these years.

"Why aren't you happy?" my mother asked, pleading more than once that I let her in on my sadness. "Where's your confidence? You don't whistle or sing anymore. You don't even smile."

I looked at her and closed my eyes. Pressed, I threw up my hands and retreated to my room without a word. Twenty, going on twenty-one, I felt like a monster, trapped in the middle of a maze. The walls made me pimpled and ugly; country, family, all those neighborhood people advising, "Nickie, wait. Patience, something good will happen." But I had no sense of an attainable happy life — as my sister Cora and even Sal apparently did. Should I remain with my parents and care for them? — Impossible. Marry Irene and raise a family? — More impossible. Write occasional songs and teach English at a nearby public high school (a career I had actually chosen in community college)? — At the time three chalkboards and a row of windows seemed like the center chamber of the most intricate maze in the world.

Strange how this situation affected our family. While it often exasperated me, I remember my parents as sympathetic, forgiving. They appreciated me more than Sal because

I had remained loyal, at home. By the time I finished my second college year, we had down-sized again to a rented one-family house in a respectable, run-down neighborhood just outside of Newark, where my mother's family lived. The newspaper-candy store had closed. My father spent more time at home, except for weekly trips to the unemployment office downtown, and the three of us felt thrown together now. I attended a different community college for extra credits and, having fewer friends, spent hours reading and day-dreaming in my attic room while my parents sat staring at the television screen downstairs. There seemed no other possible life.

"How are you doing?" one would call. "You want to come down, watch a movie?"

"I'm composing," I said, self-consciously. In truth, I sat in a rocker, smoking, staring furiously into space with the lights out. A book (war poems usually — Wilfred Owen or Siegfried Sassoon) lay on my lap as I tried to imagine myself writing the lines in it. Sometimes in an effort at talk my father trudged upstairs, knocked on the door, and very quietly, politely, asked to enter. It was one of the few situations in which I recognized his attempt to be a good father. Yet:

"Dad, I'm busy. Can't you understand?"

Resisting, he knocked again.

"With what, Nick? I can see there isn't any light on — I'm coming in."

"Dad, I'm telling you —"

Before I could finish he was in the room, clicking on the overhead light, bare bulb casting a ghastly yellow glare over everything. The smoke from my cigarette floated like a massive water flower, beige and ocher, at the ceiling.

"Oh, Jesus, can't you people ever leave me alone? Why do I —" I blinked, turning away from the overhead brightness and the slim line of his body emerging through the door. He walked over to sit on the bed.

"I'm your father. What's the matter? Can't we talk? Your mother and I both see that you're unhappy."

"I'm not unhappy. I have a lot to think about in my life."

"You mean your actress girlfriend?" My father frowned. Even in his gentle moments, he always said this with the slightest trace of scorn, as if only children — and Paolo apparently — fell in love.

I waved my hand, clever at guilt myself. "You think that's all I have to worry about, don't you? Puppy love?"

He nodded, smiling. "Lost puppy love, I suppose. At your age, is there anything else?"

"Well, I wish it was the only thing. But because of you and Mom, there are lots of other things..."

He raised his hand and sighed. "I know you didn't like this move, Nickie. I know you miss your friends ... and Philly."

He looked at me.

"It's not Philly! And it's not my friends. I'm worried about money, that's all. Who's going to support you if I leave? How are you going to live the rest of your lives without work — especially if I go away? Sal won't help. He's as good as on another planet."

My father stared — directly at me — but after a moment he shook his head and plunged on. "Well, why not tell it all? Do you want to leave? You should be able to talk about everything to me."

I grinned. I have no idea why, but with that look on my father's face images of the debonair Paolo filled my mind. On visits to the Garibaldi Club, where I drank wine with my father, played cards, and shot pool among other things, Paolo had always stood out. Above the others. And then, suddenly as I thought of that, I imagined a naked Irene strolling among the pool tables too, between Paolo and my father. I had seen my father study her when I introduced her to the family one night. I understood his gaze of appreciation. Glancing down at the poetry in my lap, I stopped in the middle of a description of a gas attack in Flanders. Irene lay on a bed of corpses, her hand out, a half-rolled rubber and gas mask dangling from her fingers. And that man, rifle in hand, leaning over her motionless body?

"Everything?" I asked, still grinning.

"Yes, everything. Are you ashamed of something?"

I nodded, looking up at him. I believed I saw through my father in those days — and all the other men at the club. Moment to moment, I never truly understood what I wanted in my life, but it annoyed me that they, especially he, understood even less. Despite the adventures and bruises he had suffered, there were times when I wondered if my father had ever been young, if he had ever wanted anything impossible.

"To be frank with you," I said, "I am ashamed."

"Of what?" He shook his head, as if relieved.

"Of you..."

He waved his hand.

"That you're my father, and you've never really talked to me. If I'm ashamed of anything, I'm ashamed of that."

"Oh, come on now, Nickie. You're a big boy now. I ain't the best of fathers, but everybody knows how proud I am of you."

"Proud..."

He nodded. "These things sort out, Nick. They always do. Sometimes after years. You're still young —"

"That has nothing to do with it! I've lived with you my whole life, and I still don't know who you are. After twenty years, you have no idea who I want to be. All I ever get is complaints about how I go out at night, how long and loud I pee when I get home, how I should join the army for the insurance or live here and support you. Making suits!"

He waved again. Embarrassed, I stared past him for several seconds, gloom and dark deepening despite the overhead bulb. I wanted to light a cigarette and blow more smoke at the ceiling but couldn't. Downstairs, the TV blared. My stomach tightened, as if someone were pulling a rope around my waist.

"Your mother and I are interested in you — you should know that. But you don't talk to us either. You've stayed home since we moved, but almost always up here. Alone. In fact you act as if you don't want to be with us at all."

"I don't!" I shouted. "I can't stand this life — this place. I don't want to follow you! I don't want to drown!"

"Please, please, Nickie! Don't say those things! They're *terrible!*"

That voice, my reader, my future, my attentive standee behind the last row, was the cry of my mother, Sophie, hitting the high C of our family troubles from the living room downstairs. I loved her more than I loved anyone at that time — more than Irene, more than Joe loved Marilyn, more than Frank loved Nancy. Yet something made me leap from the chair, open the bedroom door, and scream back while heaving my book of poetry across the room:

"Don't worry about taking care of me, Ma! — I'm the meal ticket. If you don't like the way I talk, the best thing to do is take care of yourself so I can live my own life. Which I'm going to do in any case, because I'm taking courses in that school next year — whether I get a scholarship or not. And then it's over. No more Mr. Good Son. The curtain falls."

I stared through the dark, trembling. My mother stood in her nightgown at the bottom of the stairwell, her hand clutched over her heaving breast. I flipped on the light switch and, in the sudden glare, saw a spider on a web descending toward her from the fixture above her head. My neck crawled.

"Ma, watch out — that bug! It's getting into your hair!"

With a deliberate, horrible second cry, she looked up, fell back, and slapped the spider to the floor, crushing it beneath her slippered foot. My father moaned. I looked over and saw him slumped on the bed with his head supported in his hands. The book I had thrown to the floor lay at his feet.

❖

I don't know why there wasn't any fighting after that; physical violence usually surprised our family — after a word, a petulant look, or, quite often, nothing. Sal and I had fought all the time after we moved to Philly, but never with any premeditation. That was the sadness in our relationships, and I suppose the spider took it for the whole family that night. During the intense, critical moments we turned inward, torturing ourselves with what I came to regard as puritanical guilt. My mother withdrew to her bedroom. My father, head shaking, slipped downstairs and swept up the flattened body of the spider. In the silence that followed, in the sullenness that seemed to emanate from the floor beneath my feet, I threw on a sweater and jacket, picked up my notebook and pen, and, thinking of the soldierly poets I had been reading, left the house to take the train to Philly — and my friend's apartment. No good-night or good-bye. My only comment: a glance at the carpet where death had occurred and, full of regret, a hefty slam of the door.

THE DRAGON LADY AND THE SOLDIER

I had left home and community college about a year before, you may remember, done badly the first semester and a half at the university, and dropped out, mostly because I wanted to sing songs rather than study. The following year I attended classes part time and, needing money, worked at night in a cereal factory, shoveling raw oats into a machine that shook and washed them before feeding them into a machine that formed and cooked them. My friend Will and I used to see you at a table in a coffee shop near the factory every morning. You balanced a cup of coffee in your hand, lifted your boots onto the red vinyl seat, and, with piles of cards lying like so many haystacks on the table in front of you, waited for clients. "Advice to the lovesick," we heard you say when someone asked what kind of fortunes you told. "In this town everybody wants a live-in roommate."

You also advised on tests, I remember, possibilities of military draft (this was the 1960s), professors who would be sympathetic or not, rejection or acceptance of manuscripts, football pools, problems with families, and, occasionally, job prospects and interviews when the school year ended.

"You'll never make it as a singer," you told me after I played for you one morning. "You're marking time, pining for some Catholic virgin back home."

"Marking time? You didn't like my song."

"You'll never have her."

I smiled, strumming the guitar. You glanced at Will, who frowned.

"Doubtful? — Just look at your own face in the mirror."

You shuffled the cards as if you were a gambler, dealt them with a professional slap on the Formica table top, and, almost without seeing, said something vague and general about my family, gave one or two comments about my emotional life (correct, by the way), and then offered to answer any question about it. My situation "vaguely stormy," made you smile. "You're decent but static in your allegiances, which will stop you from writing good songs." Then you added that I had an impending important event that would change my life, set me back a year or two, but in the long run free me from inhibitions.

You smiled, uninhibited yourself, I thought, and the lack of restraint was in more than your predictions. I had seen you before, during my first week at the university, coming out of the student union into the sunshine. You looked up into the sky, smiled, waved at me or others behind me, stripped down to your bandanna and what looked like bra and panties (really a thin white bathing suit, I later found out), then dove into the river that split the campus. You doggy-paddled around, came out dripping, laughing, and, long-limbed as a retriever, unashamedly put on the shirt and jeans that someone held for you. I never forgot you, but it took time to break through my "static allegiance" and speak to you because you were — in my life anyway — so different.

While I stayed in a room near campus, you rented an apartment over a garage on the other side of town. Within a week of finally saying something and hearing you tell our fortunes at the coffee shop, I spent most of my evenings and some of my nights plotting to be with you.

I was egocentric, you said, with delusions of grandeur — news to me since I felt so damned overwhelmed in your company. I would take a long, eventful trip in the next couple of years (Paris, I hoped, or some magical musician's tour), and was due for some violent knocks in the time following that would increase my waywardness but, in the long run, lead to peace and happiness.

"Take heart; something exciting will happen right here," you said during one of our morning coffees. "You're going to have an affair, a short, rather erotic one. And then that long, long journey."

You smiled, green eyes flashing. Will, seated beside me in the booth that day, gulped. A honey-haired waitress passed, holding trays loaded with cokes, burgers, and potato chips. As you, Will, and I stared at the hanging man on the card between us, I listened to the voices from the booths around us and, I'm afraid because there might be listeners, blushed.

"Who with?" I finally asked, trying to get into the proper spirit with a nervous laugh. My fingers drummed on the table.

"Most probably with a dark-haired woman. Someone from the coast." When I gave a puzzled look and drummed my fingers again, you added, "Probably me."

You were fairly close to my age, just two years older, but to my mind possessed so much more: beat up 1951 Studebaker coupe, a regular monthly allowance from your adoptive parents (Chinese immigrants, you said, who now owned a chunk of downtown San Francisco), a set of moral standards completely unencumbered by either ethnic shame or Puritanical guilt, a convenient diaphragm along with — as you phrased it during my first night in your apartment — "tons and tons of spermicidal jelly," and a rather precocious stash of pot, hashish, and silly mushrooms that you kept in an Oreo cookie box in the Maxwell House coffee can in your Amana refrigerator. All that combined with a collection of music far beyond my mostly American taste: Vivaldi, Debussy, Stravinsky. "The commercialization of everything, including drugs," you liked to say, "is the American way — to God, art, and morality. But here, in these sounds, is the presence of a spirit beyond all that. This is human intelligence. This is mind."

I understood such comments only vaguely, although I nodded knowingly when you said them. Yet there was something in your looks and attitude that made me feel comfortable and accepted — not by a girl, but by a very unusual woman.

Like me, you attended university classes, majoring in French language and culture. Unlike other students, your homework assignments weren't completed, they were surrounded on all sides and engaged. You brought me to classical concerts and museums, talked of beauty as inhaled like so much oxygen, or bitten and chewed like so much food. And in case that sounds crazy or self-centered, let me just add that you could be tender and loving with a quiet depth of feeling that no one had before or has had ever since. You moaned over stories of my parents, both of whom were grieving my abandonment of home and family back in New Jersey, sympathized with my attempts to leave them even though I had done so to escape someone you (and they) considered unworthy, squeezed my hand through the narration of our final, lugubrious farewell, and laughed with pleasure at the accounts of my family's holiday obsessions. You would listen to my groans of disgust over Kris — that Catholic virgin you had correctly seen as waiting with enormous ambivalence back home — and with what seemed like limitless patience told me that despite my fears of a dead-end romance with Kris, I did in fact have love in my future — it was, although I didn't believe you, in the cards.

"You don't know anything!" I cried, angry, even though I laughed.

"Maybe not, but you know women less. When Kris wants to get hold of you, she'll find a way. Don't forget, you're attractive. There will be others."

We might have been ironing or washing dishes together at the time, your lavender housecoat with the white imprints of Moby-Dick floating around your ankles as I stood nearby in shorts. Or, perhaps, as I circled the room, strumming a guitar, you sat cross-legged on the bed with a book, wiry, trim body looking as if it had gathered strength from jumping off steamboats. "Come on, Nick, relax. Sit next to me and enjoy the moment."

I put down the guitar but could not sit still.

"You're not going to keep yourself slim and graceful tripping around the apartment and waiting for an exciting letter."

"She's pledged to me in her way."

"Her way?" Your eyebrows rose as if they were semaphores.

"When we said good-bye, she said she would write."

You gazed around the room, sighing. "Shouldn't that mean all this — and me — is off limits? Where are your values?"

I picked up the guitar and squatted next to you. "I don't know. I don't know if I have any where Kris is concerned. Or you."

You pushed me away.

I *was* pledged, when I think of it, but on the basis of not knowing who I was. When I thought of you and especially your warmth, I thought of myself as another person — more sensual, with a fuller life. You would take me into your arms, pull at my belt buckle, and tell me to learn to live in the present. "It's gone before you know it," you said.

I would think of home, my parents, Kris, and the purer, chaster kisses I had to struggle for in my car before her family house, both conscious of her mother's eyes batting through the dark and blinds to spy on our not-so carnal ways. Your lemon breasts were not overly large, but beside my experiences with Kris they were mountains of brash obscenity that trapped me in their upper passages. On your mattress beneath the garage eaves, I would sometimes imagine dying while I stared at them, the world ending while we embraced, spinning, piece by piece, into enormous fragments while we strived to come together in a smaller, momentary peace. The guitar lay silent beside us, strings vibrating harmoniously throughout.

"Relax," you would say, as I lay on the mattress afterward, sometimes in despair, sometimes in anger, over an inability to make the happiness last. "I guarantee that I will not be in your life forever. Nor will this graceful moment."

"Moment?"

"Graceful moment."

I kissed you, somberly, began to make love again, but at some point, finished or not, I got up, marched around the apartment in desperation, then dived back onto the bed. Listening for violins with harps and guitars behind them, I tried to feel myself back to a comfortable, sensual ease.

Something — conscience, God, or, one time I thought, all my dead ancestors — stared down at me and constantly shouted *No!* You would rise, retrieve the Maxwell House can from the refrigerator, unwrap the Oreo box, and with a glass pipe that was half-bong, half-hookah, attempt to waft us over the awkward moment with soft blue smoke. Clouds of pot or hashish mixed with piano music by Satie to fill the space around us. We drifted into at least a temporary happiness, your stash the board carrying us on a magic wave into a world beyond the need for doubt.

And despite — or probably because of — all that, our conversations, usually led us back to Kris.

"Describe her to me," you said one time. "Objectively as you can."

I stammered as you put on a new cassette, babbling about her jet black hair, the showy teeth, an egregiously sad flutter in her eyelids, the categorical impossibility of doing anything immoral between those two fending hands on those two pursing lips, with that wary expression (her mother's, as well as her own) wobbling worriedly in between. You listened, intent on my eyes, and without commenting on my expression, told me I was selfish and callous, not in love at all. "You don't want her at all. You just want to break her heart."

"Heart? I want her body."

"But you won't accept her terms. Or the way she is."

It was the only time, really, that you took her side, and I'm not sure how much was in your reading of my face or words, and how much in your own experience.

"I write to her every day. And I've tried to be more than just a lover. I've tried to be her friend."

You puffed the glass pipe, stared at the cloud of smoke above us, shook your head, and glowered. "You like to day-dream and complain; you also need to make both a little exotic. Accept the simple, momentary joys, Nickie."

"What are you, a shrink or my girlfriend? What does that have to do with Kris — or us?"

And then your own anger emerged, morose, quiet, unlike anything I experienced in my own family or Kris's, with a look that brought a bitter, awful turn to your features: "It has nothing to do with us or me — quite obviously. You love no one but yourself."

You turned. Your eyes overflowed, and, helplessly, I watched you bury your face in your hands. You had a sim-ple, self-contained passion that shamed me, as if your real strength lay in this very generous fragility. Lord knows there was plenty of stubbornness in your frame. You could walk, effortlessly, faster than I could; for a mile or two you could run at the same pace as I. And you certainly could handle emotional stress and tension better than I ever have. So what to make of these sudden, un-Valerie-like tears? Why the silent misery that I could not understand, could not bear, and like a two-bit movie hero, tried in frustration to crush: Was that me, a silly Cagney, shoving grapefruit into your face one awful Sunday morning?

"Valerie, you're not being fair. You're trying to put the blame for my unhappiness with Kris on me."

But that was all I could utter before, with all those ghostly ancestors staring over my shoulder, I retreated back to my solitary, not so quiet gloom.

"You will leave me," you announced one day out of the

blue. "You will return to the life that traps you because you can not understand the world we come from. You can only think of yourself and where you've been."

Inevitably, at least during that first brief fall, we made up, embraced, and, for a while, giggled at ourselves. Then, just as inevitably, one of us (I) with hash, drink, or music playing, brought up Kris, her mother, or something else back home, and as if a bell had sounded, the fighting recommenced. Once I left your apartment and didn't return for several days. When I did return, the lights were off, unwelcoming. You huddled on a corner of your mattress, tarot cards spread in front of you, mascara on your cheeks turning your face into a Mikado mask as you whispered over and over to yourself and, I think, me, "It's ending. No matter what we do, I see everything coming to an end."

"Aw, honey, no. Forget the cards. I love you."

Your hands trembled. In sympathy I saw flames leaping across the windowpane of the dormer while a flurry of orange lightning bolts lit up the mirror beside your head. You sobbed, allowing me to hold you in the quiet of the afterglow. I'd never said I loved you before, and I could feel you were moved, though you said nothing to let me know you had heard. Silence settled, quieting the storm and the music that usually filled your room. I felt such an appealing softness in your shoulders that, despite my doubts about your predictions, an eerie chill froze my spine. Out of nowhere, as if I myself were suddenly hanging, my penis went erect against my trousers. I embraced you, feeling your breast heave against me. I kissed you again, laying you back on the mattress. You wore the lavender robe that went so well with your skin. I rested beside you, my hands straying under its hem. I felt your calves, muscular, shiver. But then I felt you kick my hands away.

"We *can't!* We're finished. Not even friends."

I kissed you again, gently. Resignation in your eyes mingled with my own fears, and I saw a strange, doomed being look out from beneath your lids. You rolled me on top of you. Before I had a chance to make any voluntary effort, you bit my lip and clutched my buttocks. I pressed against you, still seeing flames leap across the windowpane.

❖

Was it fate, cowardice, or all those ghosts at my back who made most of your predictions about us come true — at least for that particular time? I remember waking up one morning, feeling your hand beneath my buttocks, your head upon my chest, as if you were a sleeping, nursing baby. And yet (I never told you this) I suddenly perceived you as a complete and utter stranger, as if I were in a mirror staring out, and my body, in a positive-negative switch, was absolutely foreign to yours. I like to think it had to do with something in my personal past I might have better dealt with, but I'm just not sure. I remembered you saying that I would leave you, that I couldn't love you, and then that strange night in the garage when I returned, everything ended and then, just as suddenly, didn't. What did you say? — "I see everything coming to an end..."

This was mid-October, 1962, the time of the Cuban missile crisis. The very next week we heard rumors about the armed and hidden missiles close by, UN meetings with photos of them, an ashen President's announcement, and then the aftermath of the blockade, which we followed in the local bars.

I went to your apartment with Will on the night of the 24th and listened to the news on your radio as you calmly but ponderously ironed a pair of jeans. We were all apprehensive, but you were outraged, too. As the announcer described the Russian ships heading toward the Caribbean, reporting that Air Force pilots had seen unmistakable signs of atomic arms on board, you gazed darkly at the floor and started sobbing. Unclear myself, I glanced out the window and, with the twilight glittering on the houses across the way, tried to envision the landscape after a sudden magnesium-bright flash. How could a puny citizen like me prevent such things? At the same time, how could we have caused them and how could anyone have known?

"They ain't, aw shit, they ain't going to turn back," said Will, sitting on a chair near the radio and listening. "I bet we got to bomb them. I bet we got to wipe Cuba clean off the map."

He drew his thumb, fist closed, across the space in front of his neck. He was older than I, a veteran who had fought in Korea. In the coffee shop, or in the bars that often let me drink only after looking at his reassuringly mature face, he used to praise the values of military life and encourage me to get back into school full time and join the ROTC. He also talked about black outs he had experienced as a boy during World War II and the necessity for the United States to destroy any government that was not democratic. You had different ideas, of course. I could see you literally shiver at his words, wagging your head and once, after he spoke, dropping the iron loudly onto the board. For a moment the scent of your scorched jeans smelled ominous.

"Gee, do you think they'll hit here?" I asked. You nodded, eyes bright and, I saw, welcomed the thought. Will complacently waved his hand.

"Pretty near have to," he said. "If they get through. Chicago's behind us; the Air Force base is just over the county line. Paper says we're in a primary target zone."

"Jesus, I thought they'd only bomb cities. I didn't realize that this is where the hardware is."

You nodded, picking up your iron and shaking the jeans as you brushed grimly at the burn. Then you tossed them on the bed as the announcer recounted the hard-line positions Washington and Moscow presently took. Here the Army, Marines, and National Guard stood at alert; NATO forces geared up for action in Europe; and the Strategic Air

Command flew missions around the clock from Greenland through Canada. Not a moment passed without a nuclear bomb somewhere ready to tumble from the sky.

"You know," you said, "we may never see our families again. This whole continent may be wasted."

"Yup," said Will, soberly. "Theirs, too."

You shook another pair of jeans and stared at him. In a quiet, angry whisper you reminded me that we wouldn't see each other either and, nastily, began to whistle Wagner's Götterdammerung theme. Will, wiry himself, with crew-cut red hair, freckles, and an impish smile that always belied the fierce "Dragon Lady" tattoo he carried on his back, sighed. He had been imprisoned with his family in Nazi concentration camps then come to America and served in a war. In some boyish, naive way I envied that past, almost as much as I envied your knowledge of Wagner. Yet Will, just as stupidly, felt shamed by his experiences. He hated undemocratic countries, especially Russia, distrusted pimps, cities, gays, and, wrapped up in one convenient figure where independent women were concerned, you. You may have known he called you "Dragon Lady," when you weren't around.

When you asked that night how he felt about a possible nuclear war destroying everything around us, Will stubbornly shuffled his feet, eyed the sweatshirt you were ironing, and after mumbling once or twice, blurted, "Aw, Valerie, I don't know, really," several times. He shuffled his feet again before stammering at last, "Mixed up, to tell the truth. I think it's time we stood up to the Russians. They've been getting away with too much the last ten years."

"He may be right, you know —"

You looked at me, bitter, not really surprised.

"*Right?*"

I nodded. "Look at the Berlin Wall, Eastern Europe. And China. They're doing awful things over there."

"Plenty of our arms surround them, especially in Alaska and on their borders. The Monroe Doctrine?" You waved your hand. "Be real."

Will shook his head, and your expression turned to fury. You slammed the iron onto the sweatshirt, as if it were a redneck you were pinning. His face scarlet and swelling, Will said, "Bullshit, Valerie. The Monroe Doctrine don't have anything to do with it."

"Nothing?"

"No. It has to do with showing the world we aren't chicken."

"Chicken — !"

"They're enemies, aren't they! They nailed us under Eisenhower because he —"

"Enemies — ? Is it worth a civilization? Families? Us?"

I looked away, shaken, though eventually, I admit, through some backhanded logic I came to agree with Will. We had to make a stand somewhere. Why not now? At one point, Will raised his fists and shook them. "It ain't that important to me," he said. "I haven't got as many strong attachments as you — and maybe Nickie — do."

You threw the sweatshirt onto the mattress and worked on some handkerchiefs and panties. I felt embarrassed. As I sat brooding and listening to the radio, I wondered why, once again, I straddled the fence when it came to you and your opinions. Later, after Will and I left your place, I called my parents from the booth at the coffee shop, finding small comfort in hearing that they, too, viewed the situation fatalistically.

"There's nothing we can do," my mother said. "I'm not even listening to the radio. You have to live day by day."

"Moment to moment, you mean. If you hear sirens, go downstairs, please? Get under the worktable and cover yourself with blankets. Keep warm."

My mother laughed. "Warm? Oh, Nickie, if the bomb comes, I think we'll be warm enough."

"Go down there, will you? Just in case, for me?"

"Oh..."

"Mom, does Dad know where all the stuff I stored is? The radio, the blankets, the canned food? I showed it to him when I left last year. It must still be there — behind the oil burner."

Silence. My mother came back again to say, "He says he doesn't remember."

"Jesus! I showed it to him just before I left. Tell him to look for it, will you? Tonight?"

She said nothing.

"You do want to survive, don't you?"

"Oh, I guess. For what it would be worth."

"Then do what I say, Mom, for your own good."

My father came on. After I told him about the cache of supplies in the basement, he said, "Don't worry, Nickie. Everything happens for the best. You'll see."

"Only if you help it, Dad."

"And only if you come back home," he said.

Later that night you and I went downtown to a couple of our favorite bars. The sky was dark, the moon a pathetic sliver, as if it mourned the demise of a sister planet. In Labine's, where the music was usually loud and the talk animated as at a square dance, everyone was subdued, waiting for death to occur. The crowd's eyes locked onto the TV screen as bulletin after bulletin flashed news of Presidential Cabinet meetings and more Russian ships approaching the Caribbean.

"Hey, Valerie, get out the cards," the bartender said. His name was Basher. He managed to laugh, you may recall, holding a glass of beer, although the set to his eyes seemed to me distinctly nervous. "What's going to happen next?"

"This is not a joke, Basher. Though you may not recognize it, this is important in the larger scheme of things."

"If there is a larger scheme of things." Basher looked at me, winking: "We gonna get some Reds?"

You wrinkled your nose, sipping the beer he slid across the bar. "If they blow us up, at least it will get rid of shits like you."

Basher grinned. As if he hadn't heard, he pulled another draft and turned to the TV which, at that moment, showed a photograph of a fully loaded Russian ship. You stared too, I remember, and, to make sure Basher understood, tapped his shoulder and lifted your middle finger in the air. Why did my grandmother instead of you raise her finger then? And why did I, looking at you in the mirror behind the bar, see my *mother's* squared-off shoulders, the graying hair, the angry carriage of her chin, the almost cheerful superiority to all the men and boys in her life, and the looming tragedy that would unite us in death, at the same time making each of us impossible to comprehend? You lowered your glass to the bar, looking at me and saying that you had laid out your cards and read them.

"Again? When?"

"Earlier. After you and Will left. I needed to."

"And?"

Despite myself, I felt the tension in my voice.

"They show an ending, Nick. Once again."

"Really?" I looked down at the bar and, to my surprise, saw my hands tremble.

"It's an evil world sometimes, especially for you and me."

I held your hand. "If you mean I'm going to walk out on you, Valerie, especially now, I think you're wrong. If we get the time, I want to work things out."

You sipped your beer, emotionless, but with a nasty, deadly look.

"You *want* it to end," I said, "because of Kris — or something else. For your information, I didn't call her tonight. Though I did telephone my parents."

You smiled. "What's the difference?"

"It makes a lot of difference. What do you expect? Didn't you call yours?"

You shrugged your shoulders. Then you raised your chin and said it just wasn't working out between us. With others, including Basher and now Will, surrounding us and making occasional quips about Khrushchev, Castro, or the Russians, we watched the TV in silence, smiled half-heartedly from time to time as the others laughed, and finally left when, late in the night, it seemed that the loaded ships had begun to turn back. Absolution after confession, I thought; another chance to do it right.

At the garage you kissed my cheek and then, after a moment of doubt, one of the deepest I had ever seen in you, embraced me. My body stiffened. "I don't want to be tossed aside," I said. "Not now."

You shrugged, backing away. "This is youth. It'll soon be over."

"No, it isn't. It's fear — and terror," I said. "Of a life I've never wanted."

I raised my arms, but you pushed me away, crying. Should you actually propose marriage after fate miraculously saves the world? I had no clue, but you, by the look on your face, apparently had no wish for any of that. The light above the door shone brightly, casting your mouth and eyes in ghostly shadows.

"I don't want this to end, Valerie. Not ever."

"Neither do I. But here it is."

"Let's do something... Now. Right away."

Your red bandanna shook; you turned — awkwardly. Looking into my eyes, you brushed something from your forehead. "Nickie..."

I embraced you, pulling you against me with all my strength. After a moment — of real, deep softness — you pushed me away again.

Entering the apartment, you held open the door an instant and hesitated. I looked in your eyes and felt a range of things.

"Valerie, we don't have to let this happen. We can at least talk. I want to live with you. Marry you." I started to follow you, but whatever doubt you felt disappeared. You grinned, looking up at the sky.

"It'll be a long time before either of us can handle this kind of stuff, Nick. You'll come to hate yourself. You'll come to wonder what you are hating."

I brushed your hand away and tried to pull you close. "Valerie..."

"No, you'll come to *know* what you are hating. As I do now."

You spun away, decisively slamming the door as I stood there staring at your shoulders. No bombs fell from the sky, but major artillery hurtled through the ether above our heads. It would remain in motion for years. Like a man with a noose dangling from his neck, I turned, condemned, randy for life at the same time I prepared to leave it, and sprinted — across town, onto campus, up the long hill toward the dorm that in a few years would belong to a completely different kind of school: soldiers' barracks and dragon ladies with real spy missions on their minds.

It was a world that seemed, like us, to remain impeccably the same even as it was changing.

SHORT TIME

And in the end, of course, a true war story is never about war.
—Tim O'Brien

1.

"**D**id you kill anyone over there?"

I stare at my daughter, speechless, frozen into a look, a pose, that I do not enjoy, although it protects me a little from her questions while I think. "I didn't go over there to run footraces or build muscles. But I didn't take potshots at the natives either."

She nods, props her sneakers on the rungs of a chair, puffs a cigarette, even though I remind her daily that with all her exercise the smoking doesn't make sense. Mayra is not hostile, or surprised. Rather she seems to acknowledge with her look the fact that I have — what? — taken part in, fully enjoyed, even reveled in, something that, as her father, I would never approve for her and that, besides, makes smoking the equivalent of a dieter digging into a second scoop of chocolate ice cream.

"I was used," I tell her. "They trained a killer, pushed a button, and then dumped me aside when the tallies had to be taken."

She stares. "Tallies?"

"Bodies — with no thought of the bloodshed or suffering involved. They wanted a clean war they could write about in high school history books, but they encouraged a dirty one instead. And they asked us to pretend that it had been clean."

Mayra smiles, shaking out her disheveled dark brown hair. I am lucky in my daughter. With all the confusion of these past twenty or twenty-five years, with all these raps about chauvinistic men, lesbian women, violent, abusive fathers, military atrocities, the divorce case her mother won against me, bad music, drugs, and God knows what the hell goes on in schools, she's a good kid — not starry-eyed, like I was, but good. More important, she loves me, and I think I even make her proud sometimes.

"Sometimes you talk as if it was a party," she says. "As if you were just invited. Yet you volunteered; you knew what you were getting into..."

She stops.

"No. No, I didn't. You are never prepared. It's too ugly. Too awful. The daily experience is just too much. You ask yourself, what kind of life is this I'm living? Am I living?"

She turns, staring out the window on a fine spring day: snow has completely vanished, woods next to the house are greening, geese honk on a pond just a quarter of a mile away. Mayra planted crocuses outside the window last year, and a dozen or more of them bloom now, their purple, yellow, and orange cups a welcome patch of color against the muddy soil. We also turned over a garden in the back, a twenty by thirty plot of lettuce, herbs, beans, tomatoes, zucchini, and asparagus that kept me vegetarian through most of last summer and fall. She loves these things, plans to study environmental science at college next year, and dreams of a house surrounded by acres of woods. She cannot understand that fields and trees are not necessarily good for me.

"It's the life we make of it, I guess," Mayra says. "If we control it."

"If we *can* control it, you mean. You don't know what I've seen. You don't know how much loss you can sustain."

She nods. "I can imagine, Daddy." She smiles, warmly, crushing her cigarette in an ashtray as she lets out a last full stream of smoke. "Living provides the opportunity, I guess."

Her mother, Valerie, and I stopped getting along definitively the night we married. If you ask me why, I'll say it's
because we didn't really want to get married. If you ask
Valerie, it will be because I demanded too much of her time
and space. She is a social research scientist now, studying
drugs, disease, and poverty to see how they affect people's
lives. Once she cringed at scientists, believed in mind over
matter and the body's natural power to heal itself. She
wore jeans or long, loose-fitting dresses, embroidered cotton shirts with no bras or shaved armpits under them, hair
down to her waist, and loved to tell fortunes or work
through garden mud in bare feet and a straw hat that
made her look like some of the peasants I saw in Vietnam.
I was a catch for her, I suppose: We had known each other
for about a year in college and split up. I had joined the
ROTC and, at graduation, volunteered to go to Vietnam.
But upon my return there I was, for her, a vet without attitude who had come back to a college town and somehow
for those days managed to keep himself quiet while the
protests raged. For me Valerie was... I don't know. She was
something I really could not understand.

We made love — the first time in years — on my parents'
living room couch beneath a picture of cherry trees in blos-
som on the night my father, after an illness, collapsed from
a stroke. He had entered the hospital for an examination
that morning, and seemed all right, although the results
from a couple of the tests would not be clear for a day or
two. We had gone out to play cards at the Italian-American
Club, and I had picked up Valerie after staying with him
through the first couple of hands. Valerie and I went to a
movie, drank beer at a local bar, and returned to my
house. I had never brought a woman home before, let
alone make love with her in the living room. But my mother was dead. My brother Sal lived with his girl on the other
side of town. My sister Cora was married and lived with her
family. And I knew my father would stay out late at the

club. Besides, I must say, I needed the edge of danger for anything sexual to happen between me and women, especially someone I knew before, like Valerie.

Nothing had seemed right since I came back from Vietnam. I had gone on a drug and drinking binge for about a month — a period of absolute blankness in my memory — and when I came up, or out, because of Sal's, my father's, and Cora's urging, I passed weeks in a cloud of withdrawal that I hardly remember any better than the month on drugs. One day, finally, I saw where I was. As if I blinked, I looked around me, recognized I wasn't at home, realized my arms and legs were strapped down, saw the nurse in the corner dressed in neutral gray and white, and felt vaguely, comfortably, guilty, as if I had overslept, and with nothing critical missed. It took me just two weeks to leave the hospital, but it was months and months of an absolute deadness in my limbs, my thinking, my soul before I could minimally function. Writing letters helped — especially to old friends from college. And then it was a year or more — that night with Valerie beneath those painted trees — before I felt anything remotely like a normal, living need. My mother's ghost seemed to hover over us all through the hour on the couch, and the spookiness seemed confirmed when, as Valerie and I dressed around midnight, I received a phone call from the club saying my father had suffered an apparent stroke and an ambulance had taken him to the hospital.

He died just a month after that. Sal and his girl left to study in California, Cora bought a house in Connecticut with her husband, and Valerie moved into the family house with me. She is the adopted daughter of a Chinese-American, a real estate tycoon in California who had actually marched with Mao in the 1940s. She hated her father and his turncoat politics, envying him his American success since it gave her an almost impossible task of proving herself by comparison. She would gain revenge, she would make a failure of her life to make up for the aloofness and disdain he had meted out to her because she was adopted, liberal, and female. Where I fit in, I really can't say. Maybe the fact that I had fought communists, killed and maimed Vietnamese, traveled to the Orient to see and conquer... I don't know, maybe that said something to her — or to her father. For me she was in some sense a justification, and a vindication, of everything I had been — especially in Nam.

We stayed in my parents' house until the following spring when Cora, Sal, and I held a telephone meeting and decided to sell everything. We split the profits plus a few mementos, and then Valerie and I left for a month or two of wandering in Europe until that fall when "we," as she used to say, got pregnant. About to begin graduate school, she did not want the baby, and we fought about it all through the flight to the United States and the two weeks following while we looked for a hospital and doctor. We settled into our own apartment, and then immediately, brought on by the move, the fights, or the trip from Europe, suffered a miscarriage that Christmas. The experience was horrible, and there was no one to blame — not the President, not the media, not the "power structure," not the VC pigs or a stupid general. It was biology; it was God.

It changed Valerie, replaced her faith in nature with a profound distrust, and while we married, got pregnant again within six months, and then delivered Mayra in a thrilling, trouble-free Lamas style birthing room nine months later, she was never quite the same. She seemed to oppose everything, including life, after that, assault nature with strategies of chemicals, prophylactics, and sprays, until, with Mayra at last in school, she decided to return to graduate school for a degree in social work. I began graduate studies part time and, with the infant Mayra in tow, we moved to a comfortable little university town where my wife studied full time and I, between my own classes, minded baby and diapers and tried to earn a living for all of us by frying hash and eggs and bacon at the local diner. "We" got pregnant again, but Valerie absolutely refused to have it. We fought for weeks and separated. She had a change of heart, but one day in the fourth or fifth month, while I was at work, she packed her clothes and Mayra's and left town.

At the family planning clinic, they knew nothing about her, although the woman on the phone informed me that even if they did it would be highly unusual for them to tell me anything, given who I was. I drove west to Valerie's parents, following her to Los Angeles I thought, but her mother had neither seen nor heard from her in days. I went to San Francisco to see her sister, and she told me the same thing. After two weeks, I returned to my job at the diner. The police turned up nothing for several months, and then one day I received a letter from Valerie. It was postmarked from Florida, and in it she told me she had given birth to a boy and turned it over to religious authorities for adoption. She and Mayra had moved on to another state where she was working and trying to find her way back into graduate school. She and Mayra were fine, but any money I could send would certainly help. She would spend it only on what Mayra needed, none of it on herself. As always, I trusted her. I wrote out a check for twenty-five dollars and dropped it in the mail.

2.

"Anatomy is destiny," Freud said in one of his essays, tying it up, as I remember, with some other idea like the absence of a penis, the desire to piss out fire or kill your father. Other than through my reading in college, I haven't had much contact with that sort of stuff, always having loved my mother and father sincerely, never wanting to harm either, not even in a moment of anger, and never expecting any more from the plumbing between my legs than the opportunity through love or promises to extend my anatomical presence into another being, to connect with a woman if she and the moment were right, and, later, to create a child if larger, more mysterious forces than my promises agreed.

Still, I admit, I volunteered for Nam, volunteered for combat, and took pride that of the hundreds of thousands over there, I was one of the rare, and I must say privileged, thousands to have gone out on the hunt for fire. There were three kinds of grunts in Nam: the reluctant ones who regretted every moment in the field; the eager who loved to fight to make something of themselves, or to make up for something missing in themselves; and the rest, a narrow majority, I believe, who simply went out to fight because they loved their country, this was war, and they had the quiet faith to know that, win or lose, they could do it, not greatly, but well. And that was how I saw myself: average, caught up in a world turning ugly against my wishes. My father had not fought in World War II; he had worked in a defense-related industry instead. None of his brothers had fought, and his radical father had joined some sort of pacifist, socialist alliance that somehow made him unfit for World War I in Italy. And my own brother, Sal, god knows, had done everything short of crossing the border to avoid the war. Whatever he did, it worked. Once he registered at seventeen, he never even heard from our draft board again, not in 1965, not in '68 (a year after I left for Vietnam); not in 1970 or later, when the draft lottery went into effect.

So, unlike a lot of guys I met in country, I had no pressure to join up from a family tradition. But the feeling was in there, inside me, whether from books, movies, or TV, I'll never know. I just felt that I had to go, as if I owed something. Call it my anatomy if you will, but I thought I'd never be happy with myself if I stayed home. I could have taken a job helping the poor (plenty of my friends had done that), or gone to graduate school, earned another degree, and taught. Instead, I saw an image of me in combat boots and fatigues with a rifle in my hand, and despite all the doubts of my mother and Cora, the laughter and scorn of my brother Sal, I felt I needed to make that image real. And it was more than feeling and need. It was knowledge and inevitability. I had no idea what came after that bright, self-contained image I saw, but it was a self that would continue to torment me whether I wanted it to or not (I didn't want it to). More important, I knew it as the most positive image of myself I would ever see.

To my surprise, and for one of the few times in my life, my imagination was right: I turned out to be a damn fine soldier, one of the kind a company depends on, the kind his fellow soldiers respect and his commanders like. I volunteered for search and destroy, rescue missions, and reconnaissance. I marched quietly, tending to business, never hot-dogged or otherwise blew the company's cool. I received commendation for valor twice, led my units with a minimal loss of men and a minimal loss of discipline among the men, and so when Tet hit in early 1968, mine was one of the few company units not to lose a man, not to give up a foot of turf when the fire erupted in our zone.

I still wonder about it. Freud says men are natural killers and rapists, I think, holding back their aggression to build cities and nations, to write songs and shape their futures. But what about us, and there are many, who give in to their anatomy for a period in their lives, or for a moment, and somehow see a different vision? That morning of Tet, a quiet, warm dawn, as I recall, with clouds above the mountains turning the sun into a ghostly lavender shade, erupted into a battle that didn't stop (for me) for several years. Camped in a field near a village not many miles from the mountains, I walked through some thick brush toward a river I could wash in and, as I had the day before, stopped on this little pile of red earth to look at the sky. It was dangerous, but we had cleaned out the zone a week before. Besides, I love the morning, always feel secure in it, and felt an inner need to stand on that hill, turn a circle with a rifle and canteen in my hands, and take it all in: the conical mountains, the wide gaps between them, the village lights on the fields to their left and right, the lush growth of trees and brush behind me, and a single, narrow gap, this one through the trees, of a path on the way to fresh water.

"What a morning!" I whispered, seeing the mountains, the trees behind me, and the lavender light just spreading across the clouds and sky like a huge drop of ink mixing with a bowl of water. I heard a rustle to my right, dropped to one knee, and raised the rifle to see a little village dog, white, short-haired, with a black patch over one of its eyes, emerge from the underbrush and after a short stop head straight up the hill toward me. I studied the brush to its left and right, and behind me, seeing no other movement. It paused about ten feet away, swinging its head to the right and wagging its tail as if to ask my permission to come closer. It was thin, obviously underfed, with ribs prominent through its skin. I studied the brush again, feeling terribly vulnerable in that place, and, not wanting to make too loud a sound, waved the barrel of the rifle to send the dog away. It whimpered, lay down, and rolled over as if by my command. On its feet again, it stepped closer, wagging its tail and staring into my eyes as if begging me to take it in. I waved the rifle again, and this time it lay on its back and wagged its tail. I walked down the hill toward the gap in the trees and, rifle ready, headed for the water.

The dog ran ahead, obviously knowing the trail, and, with stops to sniffle and pee, led me into the brush until we were surrounded by trees and shade. I was spooked, I admit, feeling the dog was a trap, leading me somewhere I didn't want to go, even though it headed in the same direction I had intended. A warm breeze blew through the dark brush, and I kept reminding myself that we controlled the area. We had cleaned it out just two days ago and were, definitively, in charge. No one unfriendly should have been within a mile without me knowing it. Of course you know, as I did then, that by the order of some fun-loving, or hateful, god, thinking like that often leads humans into trouble.

The path led directly to the river. The dog followed it, stopping as we got to the banks to sniff at a stump and the rump end of a pile of wood. I glanced around, rifle still poised, and emerged from the overhang of trees. Like so many rivers I had seen in Nam, this one flowed muddy and deep, and there were times when the men really didn't want the water. But a few feet from the banks, the water flowed more clearly, and so, if you felt lucky, you could risk finding something better.

Just out from the brush, I looked at the trees across the way. Even with the sun behind me, shining into those trees, I saw nothing, and with the dog sniffing at the trees and stump without suspicion, I decided to take the chance, especially since I knew the bank wasn't steep at all. Fully clothed, with the rifle and canteen above my waist, I slipped my boots into the water, sank into the mud until I found a couple of stones to stand on, and then, resisting the current, gradually strode down and along the embankment until, about twenty-five feet out, the river rose to my armpits. Water ran clear out there. As I lowered my canteen into it, I looked around: The sun shone above the trees behind me now; near the banks of a little peninsula down river a silver-colored bird, a crane or heron probably, stood in the water, one foot lifted, and seemed to listen for movement. It dunked its head, came up with nothing, and, after a sidelong glance at something on the peninsula, spread its wings and lifted off. Spooked myself, I waded back toward land, scanning the landscape on either side of the river, and feeling only slightly more comfortable when I saw the dog still at its original spot.

Dripping, I capped the canteen. I had lost nearly a quarter of its contents on the way back but didn't care. I took cover in the trees, stopped at the edge of the clearing to glance around, and still saw nothing. Another water bird, light turning its silver colors golden, grazed near the opposite shore now, and I started back for the camp after another few minutes of staring. The dog ran ahead of me and led the way. We came to a fork in the road that I had often wondered about. One path led back to the camp, and the other I didn't know. I had followed it for a few yards once on reconnaissance and knew that it was overgrown, winding through a marshy, open field with hills on either side. I didn't know where it led, although I suspected, from our maps, that it turned back to the original path. The dog took the fork, stopped when I looked after it and hesitated, and then simply put its nose to the ground and plunged on. I took the original way but, after a few steps, felt I shouldn't. What kind of officer wouldn't completely know the territory he and his men guarded? What kind of security did we have if I didn't know this path between two dots in our recon packs?

Without thinking further, I turned, making sure my rifle was dry, and plunged after the dog onto that second path. The woods and brush were thicker here. The path curved off to the left, skirted a paddy, and, muddy there, pointed toward some other woods where it entered the trees and brush again. I saw no new footprints, no sign of life except the dog and its paws. But as we moved closer to the trees, another path crossed this one from the direction of the river, and at that junction I saw fresh human prints, not from Marine-issue boots but retread tire sandals that must have turned outward with each step, scooping up a delta of mud and clay with the arch side of the sandals. I felt myself crouch automatically, keeping the rifle ready at my chest, and followed slowly, quietly as I could, behind those prints. I heard nothing, not a voice, not the sound of any animal. The dog dropped back a few steps, its nose closer to the earth as it sniffed each little mound the sandals left, and then as we walked beneath the trees, glanced back at me and darted forward. I took two or three steps to follow, arrived at a curve, crouched lower as I took two more steps, and saw the back of a man in front of me, walking in the same direction.

His shoulders slumped forward, his head inclined toward the mud he trudged through. He wore black pajamas, a straw papa-san hat, and seemed to carry something, I wasn't sure what, in his arms. The dog caught up with him, barked, circled his feet, and leaped on his hip with great delight. I fell to my knee, seeing the man stop and turn toward me. He moved quickly. I saw the dark barrel of his rifle — almost lost in the darker cloth of his pajama top — and with my own M-16 already at my shoulder, I centered the hairs on his chest and squeezed the trigger.

3.

"Blown away," the Top said to me. "Completely. But you had to do it. How could you tell?"

I had run back to the hooch, still seeing the surprised look, the hat flying like a conical saucer, the pajama top exploding with the blood, the frail body lifted out of its sandals and almost out of its trousers, and the dog, wailing, plunging into the underbrush, running evasive patterns through the trees. After a few seconds, I retreated to the clearing and, on my stomach, checked out the paddy and the hills beyond. I saw nothing. Returning to the body again, I took another look along the path and through the trees. Again, nothing. I looked down, saw the legs twisted as if to run in the opposite direction of the trunk, and then, checking for identification, I noticed two things: the "barrel" didn't extend from a rifle but was a farm tool, a hoe of some kind, and the "chest" I had blown out of its shirt held the remnants of two breasts with a woman's nipples on them.

Later, I sat on my cot with my head in my hands and tried to understand what happened. I knew I had acted properly, although perhaps a little hastily, and that even a peasant woman might have been dangerous, armed or not, because she might give information to others. But I had been very careful up to that point, keeping the men of my platoon under tight control, never allowing them to take the slightest chance on injuring peaceful people, men as well as women. I had succeeded in keeping our record clean of any atrocities, and in fact, despite the snide remarks of a couple of my regulars, I had impressed on the men the need to represent our country well: "If we're fighting to make them friends," I told the men, "we damn well have to make them *want* to be our friends, especially while we're fighting on their land."

And I had done well, proud of my platoon's record in battle and my own record as their leader. You've heard the stories. The burned villages are nothing, almost excusable, because in fact the men couldn't know what was hidden inside the huts, or beneath them. The personal, individual injuries were worse: Soldiers taking target practice at peasants working in a field; grunts forcing grenades down a valuable working cow's throat; men viciously raping whole families of women and then killing them. Those are the stories we've brought back, admit to. For every one of those there must be hundreds unreported and, maybe, worse.

But I had steered clear of that as best I could, made my men avoid it too. Yet now, as if it were a mine, I had stepped onto it by accident. We controlled the area, but by no means knew all the people in it. So it was hard to know who this young woman was, whether in fact she lived around here, and if, as my gut said she did, she had a family. I wanted to make retribution, pitiful as that might seem, and so, after a half hour or so in the hooch, I left the Top in charge and walked back to the overhang to look around.

At the path I saw no new footprints, just the narrow bump, bump, bump of the little crescent moons her sandals had left. Blood had drained from her. Flies cruised from her mouth to her wound, to her nose and then her wide-open eyes. Without thinking, I looked at her hands, but I had never seen a ring on any of these people, married or not. She carried no papers, and when I looked inside her clothes and hat, even at the hoe, I found no writing, nothing to identify her in any way.

I continued along the path, hoping to find a field, a hut, or possibly a little village. Unlike the first trip, I felt no fear, not even a sense of caution. I might have walked into a minefield for all I knew. But, even at a step away from losing everything, I could only see that woman's face when I shot her. Sometimes I thought of Cora, sometimes of my mother, and once or twice, with irony, I thought of my brother Sal, of the smart remarks he might make.

The path went through a paddy, skirted another overhang of trees, passed a muddy, foul-smelling field, and led up to a group of five or six huts that we had not known about. Three men and a woman in black pajamas worked in a paddy just beyond the huts, and a couple of older women watched some kids playing behind them. I walked slowly, rifle up, but reluctantly, watching the huts, and hoping to make some kind of peace with these people without the ground blowing up beneath my feet. The two older women stopped talking and stared at me. Then the kids stopped, and one of them called out to the men and woman in the paddy. Slowly, I took a white handkerchief out of my pocket and waved it. They did not respond. As I came closer, the two men in the paddy walked toward the huts, arriving near the old women and children just as I did.

"Hello," I said.

"*Howa*," one of them said, a mix, as I imagined it, of "hello," "hi," and "how." One of the men, obviously nervous, waved his hand. I have read a good deal about how beautiful the Vietnamese are, but very little about the hardness you can see on their faces. It's a look that says they expect nothing and will give nothing, having nothing to give or expect. They work hard. We used to see them bending over the paddies for hours, never standing straight as they walked from rice plant to rice plant all day long, dawn to sunset. They speak little, even among themselves, at least when strangers are around. So, the man's nervous show of friendliness made me wary. "GI welcome," he said. "America number one."

Holding up a thumb, he laughed, and the whole group of them did the same.

"Are you all here?" I said, trying to sound official. "Anyone missing?"

The man frowned, eyeing the rifle and my lieutenant's stripes. The four of them fell into a conversation I could not follow. They pointed in several directions at once, waved their hands, said "Number one" a couple of times, and, finally, the smiler shook his head.

"Woman gone ... hoe?" I said, raking at the ground with my rifle butt.

They shook their heads, unsmiling. "No hoe," one of the older women said and shook her head again. A crane circled overhead, its neck in an s-curve, its legs dragging behind as if on a separate current. For a moment we all studied it, and then the smiling man touched my sleeve, raising his hands when I quickly stepped away. "American GI," he said, raising his thumb again. "Number one."

I took his sleeve, trying to look sincere, friendly, and in charge at the same time. "Come," I said. "You come with me." He looked at the others, shrugged his shoulders, and raised his hands. But he didn't budge. He and the others talked and the women shook their heads. I tugged his sleeve again, not letting go this time, and made sure to pull him with me as I walked. The other man and the two women followed, first sending the children into the fields where the lone woman and man stood and watched, motionless.

We followed the path through the overhang, past the

two paddies and the smelly field, and came to the overgrown path where the woman lay. The four of them
remained silent, as I did, their eyes wide but not fearful,
their behavior remarkably composed, I thought, considering that I carried the rifle. Occasionally they whispered
something to each other. It was nothing that I could
understand, but at the same time they showed little sense
of fear, even as we turned a bend and saw that body
sprawled out about sixty yards ahead. At that point the
four of them stopped, looked quickly at each other then at
me. Their expressions changed, but I could not really say
how. Maybe it was just the responsible, final presence of
the dead. Probably it was more personal. The serious man
whispered something to the others and all four forged
ahead. The women went first, the men lagging behind, but
all just ahead of me as I followed and made 360-degree
turns with my eyes and the M-16. They ran for a bit, talking quickly, then stopped about ten yards away from the
body and, silent again, circled it.

"Do you know her?" I said. "From your village?"

They stared at her a long time, not saying anything to
each other or me. The smiling one covered his eyes and
looked away. One of the old women spit into the dirt near
the corpse's foot and rubbed her hands together. The other
woman, with an incredibly strong, if wrinkled face, shook
her head. I looked hard into the thick brush, saw no sign
of that spotted dog, and, loudly, asked them again if they
knew her. I mentioned the dog, but that said nothing to
them. The serious one began to speak, but when he saw I
didn't understand anything raised both his hands and
repeated "G.I. number one" several times. All four repeated that, the women less convincingly, I thought, and when
one of them looked down the path behind me, I spun
around and dropped to one knee. With my rifle at my
shoulder, I saw one of the little kids. But before I could do
or say anything, the two old women fell to their knees in

front of me and tried to grab the M-16 barrel. The two men patted my shoulders and made me understand that nothing was wrong, at least nothing worth shooting a rifle over. They smiled, trying to point the barrel into the air. Furious, I stood, shoved the rifle in the smiling one's face and, telling them to stop, made them all raise their hands above their heads. I felt scared, super, super spooked. I did not like all those people surrounding me. Backing away, I started toward the river and the camp. Passing the corpse, I reached into my pocket and, half wanting to rub their noses in it, pulled out some coins and threw them on the ground. They said and did nothing. I continued to back away, staring into the brush and hills all around, and finally, at the bend where I had seen her, turned and ran. The last thing I saw was the child in the smiling man's arms and the strong, wrinkled woman on her knees before the corpse. She wasn't gathering money. With her hand to her face, she bobbed her head forward and backward, almost touching the ground. I thought I heard her scream.

4.

That afternoon the VC hit us with everything: mortar, rocket shells, rifle fire. As we set up defenses to repel them and reconned to try to track them down, the earth shook beneath our feet, trees exploded, the night sky turned treacherous as mud, rock, and roots plunged over and around us, as well as through some unlucky others. The attack made us forget everything except the most primitive responses — dip, dodge, dive, the muscular descent into darkness and security. I forgot that woman and her death, I forgot that family of peasants and my coins. For a certain time I also forgot who I was — name, serial number, everything. But I am a little ashamed to say that my sense of rank and responsibility never left. I kept my men together, gave clear directives, made them act orderly even under stress, forcing them to remember that we were Marines, American Marines, and as such had an important job we could not foul up, especially now.

They responded beautifully, as I knew they would, calling in mortars and air strikes of our own, securing the area within three hundred yards of the camp, and knocking down a verifiable eighty-five or one hundred of the enemy within forty-eight hours. I have read that the VC Tet offensive of 1968, militarily, at least, was a failure, and I can only say that according to what I saw and experienced that assessment is accurate. Our company gave no quarter, lost no territory, almost no equipment, and very few men. In addition to the ones we killed, we captured more than fifty of the VC themselves. Toward the end of the first three days, I began to look at enemy faces again, hoping to catch a glimpse, for self-justification, of one of the village peasants I had left on the trail. But, in all honesty, I think I had already forgot what they looked like. I could never pick anyone out. What's more, I never got back to the village to see how they were because, although I reported the presence of that village and the killing of the woman in the path, our platoon never had the time to march into the area and control it, at least not under my command. About three weeks after the attacks began, when things were mostly under control again and we were pounding butt to keep things orderly on the new LZ, we received orders to recon that village. My platoon was leaving that very afternoon, after a morning of loading supplies, but then the Top walked up to bring me another, uglier, piece of news.

"Lieutenant, sir."

"Top. You're not bringing me new casualty figures, I hope. I'm tired of them."

"No, sir."

"Or new offensive plans. God knows we're hurt enough as it is. I don't even want to go out into the field."

"No, sir. No new plans."

"Discipline?"

"It's nothing like that, sir. Nothing military at all."

"Good, cause I'd just as soon hear about the Phils or the Pirates as goddamn VC today."

The sergeant lowered his head and shook it. "Nothing like that either, sir, I'm afraid."

I glanced over at a dusty six-by rumbling toward us with supplies — food, equipment, the thousands of rounds of ammunition we spent every day — even without the VC attacking us in waves. "Well, what is it then?"

He said nothing. I watched the six-by driver pull to a halt, backing up to the doors of the Chinook. Some men put down their rifles, others turned about, staring alertly into the jungle for any unusual movement.

"Well, Top, what is —"

I glanced at him and saw his arm extended, a folded piece of yellow notepaper in his hand, "Red Cross" stamped on top. He continued to look down at his feet as I took the paper. I unfolded it, read the message, and waved to the six-by driver, pointing to a load of containers I wanted brought back. When he gave me the okay sign, I read the message again: *"Mother dead. Prepare to leave immediately."*

"I'm sorry, sir."

I said nothing, wondering if it wasn't some bad company joke. I was on what we called "short time"; my combat duty was coming to an end, and I was ready to leave the war in another fifteen days. I checked the Top for a smile, but saw only his long, serious expression. Nodding, I thanked him for the news and asked when the message had come in. "Within the hour, sir. I brought it right over from the CQ. Captain says he'll get you out on the first helicopter he can. Jones will take over here, sir. You're to come right back with me."

"The war is over," I said.

He looked at me strangely.

"Can you wait a minute, Top?"

"Sure, Lieutenant. Whatever you like."

Thanking him, I walked toward the six-by, picked up some gear I had stashed near the Chinook, and after a quick, unsatisfying farewell to the men in my platoon, rode back to CQ with the Top Sergeant. There, the Captain informed me that a copter would leave for Saigon in an hour and emergency orders would be waiting for me there.

I went to the hooch, packed my gear, said good-bye to some friends, and within an hour was in a Chinook, hearing the ping of sniper fire against the fuselage and blades as they lifted us over the mountains and carried us south along the river. I said nothing to the crew. But they must have known something; they maintained a respectful silence as I looked out the window and, from time to time, glanced at the last letter from my mother. "At last," she had written, "it's decided. I'm going into the hospital next weekend and I'll have the operation on the following Monday. I want to get this over with so I can be well when you come home. Just two more months! If I get the operation now, the doctor says I'll be well enough…"

I had received the letter just a few weeks before, on the morning before Tet. I had worried a little; but from the tone of my mother's letter nothing dramatic seemed imminent. I was in a period of my life where I tried to minimize worry where my loved-ones were concerned. My mother had not wanted me to join up; my father had. I had been sheltered, but now that I was twenty-two, had seen battle and, indeed, killed, I felt that if I let myself become frightened over my mother's health, I would never leave her in any permanent sense. I had the habit of suppressing feelings in relation to her, had joined the Marines as part of a personal campaign to cut the apron strings, "become a man," as we liked to say, and so, as I read her last letter on the way into Bien Hoa, I suppose I kept myself from feeling its effect. Instead, I concentrated on that woman, and the family, becoming resolved in some way that I had done the right thing. As I stood in the sun at the airport while waiting for my plane, I acted quietly sorry but, looking back on it now, pretty clear-headed. It just didn't seem real — neither my mother, nor that woman. The dead were torn apart, burned, suddenly shot as they popped a lude — or they were simply blown away during an act of carelessness. There was nothing you could do but try. It was a zone of happenstance. I had survived, others hadn't. But there would come a war, hot or cold, that would get me too. So I was detached, occasionally even buoyant at my good fortune that afternoon as the plane left the cement and metal of Saigon and leveled off over the Indian Ocean, carrying me toward America where, in less than forty-eight hours from the time the Top Sergeant held out the note, I stepped off the bus in my hometown.

Tired and relieved, I walked the two blocks from the bus station, stood a few minutes before the dark house, and, finally, rang the bell. I had to ring it a couple of times, knock once, and call out beneath a window in back before the lights went on. My father, in his undershorts, answered the door.

"Hi, Dad. How are you?"

"Oh, Nickie..." He waved and let me into the living room before saying anything else. My father always struck me as absurd in his underwear; now, after three years of khaki and more than one of blood he seemed less so. He had a lanky body with thin arms and legs, and a bulky middle dominated by a firm paunch whose size amazed people, including himself. He attributed the firmness to indigestion — gas, which, he claimed, forced him to emit enormously loud farts that, with a chuckle to this day, I remember as rifle shots or grenade explosions. He had a standard story, told over and over through my youth, that he was born farting instead of crying, and that his mother said it had saved his life when he had colic. He wore boxer shorts and strapped

t-shirts as a rule, and his shorts flapped like a clown's pan-
taloons when he walked, so that any bravado he had always
lost force by the memory of him stripped to his underwear.

"Are you alone?" I asked. "Cora isn't here?"

"Naw, she went home to the kids. Sal is here — in your
room."

Sal, my younger brother, was twenty years old, already
working and living on his own — and attending college. He
would be the one to spend time with my father, I thought.

"Dad, tell me ... what happened?"

He waved again and turned to sit on a chair. I glanced
around the living room, immediately feeling uncomfortable. The room was decorated completely to my mother's
taste. There was an old flowered sofa, a French provincial
coffee table, a leather-topped lamp stand that sat in the
middle of a picture window, and that large, idyllic print of
blossoming cherry trees with a gaudy, gilded frame. The
print showed a small brook behind the trees with grass on
each bank, and pink on pink of blossoms covering the
grass, sky, and brook, turning everything else into background. It was slightly religious at the same time it was
vacuous, and I'd often recalled it with irony when we
marched into darkly foliated jungles back in Nam.
Vegetation was a trap back there. Here, within a frame, it
gave our living room a sense of peace and space.

Dropping the duffle bag to the floor, I bent over my father,
and embraced him, even though he tried to push me away.

"Don't," he said, letting his arms settle across his stomach. "Those goddamn doctors did us dirty."

He sat next to his desk, a tall secretary he had inherited from his father, and let his face fall into his hands. My
stomach turned. He needed strength, I know, but as if I
were speaking to a new recruit, I told him to buck up and
be brave. The enormity of the situation had not fully
touched me yet, I think, and when I tried to calm him in
firm, soldierly tones, it only made him moan. Then the look

on his face grabbed me at the heart.

"I — I'm sorry," I managed to blurt out while I looked at him. "I — I'm —"

He waved his hand, as if to push it all away. "We're all sorry. That was the best goddamn woman —"

There was real loss in his grief, and as his sobs smothered his words, I waited a few seconds, looking around the living room and wished I could push everything away. "Christ," I said at last. "I haven't seen a bed in two days. Can we talk about all this in the morning? I need a break."

He turned on the stairway light and allowed me to walk with him to his bedroom. When I went upstairs to my own room, the darkness seemed to close in on me. I sensed that the excitement I had been having for the past three years — or at least my feeling of excitement — had been youthful imagination. I had thought I was leaving something behind, that I might get hurt but at least I would be different. Yet as I turned on the small lamp in my room and saw my brother Sal in the twin bed next to my desk, I had the feeling that things were really staying the same. A car rolled down the street; in the distance I heard something that sounded like gunfire. I took off my clothes, whispered hello as Sal, turning and briefly looking my way, threw up a sleepy wave. I noted the long hair, the beads around his neck, and the unshaved woolliness on his chin. I turned off the light, smiling. Without thinking about it, I pulled the covers from the bed and, wrapping myself up in them, lay on the hard wood floor.

5.

Despite my memories, I understand little of that period. My daughter, Mayra, seventeen, beautiful in spite of chopped and lacquered hair, insists that I have gone nowhere, that I "simply do not see," as she says it, and that for her no war is worth death, no death worth a life, no life worth the heartbreak that went into maiming it. "Child of the new century," she calls herself, meaning that she is used to separation, the independence that comes from lack of family, the superficial sense that she and her peers are just one big — not necessarily happy, but very separate — world.

"Touchy-feelie," she calls me — the sexual meaning secondary in her words. "I mean *feeling*. You and your people are always trying to emote."

She grins, her dark eyes (from her mother) sparkling, her nose in the air (also from her mother), her shining hair spiked and messy as she laces a pair of pumped-up workout shoes.

"'My people?' Who do you mean by that?"

She nods. "You know. Sixties, seventies. 'All We Need is Love', 'Let's Do it in the Road.' It's all so innocent — and phony."

She laughs, stretching her legs as she rises, her haunches tight while she leans against my father's old desk chair. I can't stand the thought of her with men, especially boys her own age, the ones with clowny pants and shoes and designs razored into their hair. I worry about AIDS, pregnancy, rubbers that somehow fall apart or disappear.

"Don't break that," I say, pointing to the chair. "Loosen up on something stronger."

She switches to the wall and, after a minute stretching out each calf, walks to the front door. She is going to jog to a club I bought her a membership in and workout with an aerobics class. Her boyfriend will meet her there, pump himself up with the hardware my membership pays for, and, I am sure, in the wee, small hours of tomorrow morning, get naked with her before he drives her home. "I'll be careful," she says, before I can voice my caution. "I will stay away from cars, keep to the better lit districts, and not workout beyond my strength. I will keep warm, dry, and clean, and I assure you that Darth will use a condom. But you have to remember that some of that depends on mood."

She opens the door and stares into the evening. The sun has turned colors in the clouds above the trees. "Like lollipops," she says, stretching her arms out toward the horizon. "I want to take it all in."

"Tomorrow," I say. "Tomorrow night I want you to stay home with me."

She nods. "Is Darth invited?"

I nod. "If he wants to see the film."

"Film? Oh, God, the film I've been hearing about for years? I'm not sure what you want me to see."

"How we were."

"I've seen that before. Often." She frowns.

"No, you haven't. Not with my family. I want you to know. Then maybe next day I'll take you to the grave."

"Grave?"

"You know, your grandparents. You've never been there. I want you to see it."

She makes a face, runs her fingers through her hair, and puts on a pair of cotton gloves. Then, without so much as a nod, she steps into the twilight and closes the door. Who knows what men are down those lanes, among those trees, lying in wait for her with rage and death in their arms? I run out to the sidewalk, step into the driveway, and, my heart pounding in desperation, put up my hand and wave.

6.

Our family was not given to open displays of affection. We did few things together, and since my parents were not church-going Italian Catholics, we didn't even worship together. Bursts of anger and exasperation were more habitual than affection, and the only time I remember real, extended, joyful contact between my mother and father

was at their twenty-fifth wedding anniversary, significant-
ly an event that was captured on film and more significant
perhaps because it was the one time I ever saw my father
drunk. He was so drunk, in fact, that he had to leave the
party early to go to bed, where he vomited and nearly
choked himself to death. The only direct memory I have of
the time is my father, pale and groggy, hands trembling as
he tried to drink coffee next morning, his face whiter than
the sugar on the doughnut he habitually dunked into his
cup, and my mother, hardly sympathetic, warning me
never to let myself drink that much.

The movie of that evening is different, and that is why I
have wanted to show it to Mayra for so long. It is black and
white, about fifteen minutes long, on cassette now with no
sound or editing. The party was held in the basement of
the huge two-family house that Sal, Cora, and I sold many
years ago, only to see it knocked down to make way for
condominiums.

My parents had bought it in 1949, and my father had
remodeled part of the basement into a recreation and party
room. It contained a ping-pong table, a couple of couches,
and two rows of benches along the walls. There were pictures of movie and sport stars on one wall, and a coconut
painted to look like an Indian beside them. The anniversary film opens with a shot of the coconut, moves along the
wall to a picture of Joe DiMaggio and, beside him, one of
Lana Turner, then pans the room to photograph the family and guests. I'm chubby and cute in my shoot'em up
cowboy hat and holster; Sal is smiling and sweet in his little Peter Rabbit pajamas; and Cora is sparkling and beautiful in her curly Jane Russell hair. Almost everyone, close
and distant from the family was in attendance, and the
camera registers all of them as it pans matter-of-factly,
stopping at the far end again, where the table is now laid
out as the party's centerpiece. There, beneath the picture

of Joe Di and Lana, my mother and father stand in front of the anniversary cake. "Nick and Sophie, Twenty-five years," the camera tells us, "Happy Anniversary."

My father holds up the cake while the camera zooms in and back; then he sets it on the table and, taking a sly look at my mother, sticks his finger into the frosting and licks it off. She slaps his hand, and to the shouting and laughter that must have followed, he grabs her shoulders and plants a creamy, frosting-layered kiss on her mouth. She shoves him away, wiping her mouth. He kisses her again to, what I gather from the looks on their faces, is general merriment.

My mother takes a knife, slices it expertly into the cake, cuts the first piece, and lifts it out to feed my father. His eyes shine confidently, glint naughtily in a way that shows he knows his manner pleases. He takes a section of the piece and feeds it to my mother — who baked the cake, I believe, although it was Aunt Carol who probably did the decoration. When my mother bites the cake, she makes exaggerated, smacking motions with her lips. The camera shows her as plain, with premature gray hair combed straight back from her forehead, and, because of her shame over two missing front teeth, a close-lipped smile. Whatever the reason, the film shows clearly that although I remember her strength and sobriety throughout our life, and eventually tried to copy it, my father was the free-spirited, attractive one having a good time. That's all: a few cheap feels from him, he laughs; a few embarrassed, tight-lipped smiles from her, and I still feel my heart stop (and see the note the Top put in my hand) when the movie ends abruptly in a shower of light: My mother cuts the cake. We see it passed out to the rest of the party as snow begins to dot the screen, spreads, sticks, and eventually, before one bite is taken, turns it white.

I had mixed feelings as Sal drove my father and me down to the funeral home the day after my arrival. The undertaker was a man I had known since elementary school. He had always been a skinny, ratty looking boy, and because of his family's business we used to call him "Digger," or "Digger Di," although his family name was simply Maggio, after the month of May. Young, neat-looking that morning, he wore glasses, carried himself bent slightly from the waist, his hands folded before him as if he anticipated something with pleasure. He showed us the viewing room, and to my relief said my mother "was not ready," but we could see her that afternoon. He also told us that my mother's favorite priest, Father Peter Rossi, would be there and that he would conduct a service for her. I said nothing then, but secretly I felt numb. I had for so long seen life as cheap, not really to be desired, and I felt that funerals, especially those with religious services were hypocritical. Sure it was tradition, family, Catholic, and Italian, but I had seen a different world and wanted it recognized by the others. It wasn't until Cora arrived that afternoon to talk over arrangements with Sal and me that I said anything.

"Why do we need a priest? Why can't we just wrap her in a blanket and bury her in the backyard, or cremate her?"

"In the backyard? Are you crazy?" Cora said.

"Dad wants it this way," Sal said. "They were raised in the Church, married in it, so..."

"Oh, God, why do we need *anything*? If we need a sermon, why can't it be given by one of us?"

"Nickie, if you want to say anything, go ahead. But it better be pleasant. Everybody thinks a religious ceremony is appropriate. And certainly no cremation."

Sal nodded. "Mom was loved, after all, and, thank god, this isn't Vietnam."

I looked at him, my fists clenched, and I swear, although

we had not said an angry word in years, I was one syllable away from choking him. Sal's hair, and particularly his unshaved chin, looked terrible. Cora touched my shoulder and said the decision was not really ours, but our father's. "He wants it," she said. "Her family wants it." She looked at me. "Sal wants it, and I want it, too."

"Forget it," I finally said, unclenching my fists.

"Forget it? What — that she ever lived!"

Cora closed her eyes and tears rolled down her cheeks. Sal glared at me, taking her in his arms with soft moans and whispers. He stared at me over her shoulder, his eyes wet and red as Cora's, his jaw set and grim. "It *has* changed you," he said, quietly, looking at my uniform. "Well, it doesn't mean you know everything. It doesn't mean the change is for the better."

I said nothing. I stared at Cora, who stood huddled within his arms, and remarked to myself how slim she had become. Living in New York with her husband, Hank, she had begun to lose some of that natural, Jane Russell heft and develop a slim, more tailored figure. Solemnly, an older, more loyal sibling than either of them (I thought), I walked away, ignoring them both when they called my name.

I admit that during the next three days I began to have a change of heart. Walking around the house or the neighborhood, seeing the family at the funeral home, I searched for significance and felt along with Sal and Cora that something had to be made of my mother's passing. Despite all that I had seen recently, I could not stop a religious prayer from parting my lips when I first looked at her in the coffin each afternoon. She looked waxen, small. I saw myself in her dead body, thought about friends I had already lost, and didn't want to accept the frustration of her death as being her only end. Why had I survived so far? Why hadn't others? I kneeled before her casket, waiting for something to transform the sense of decay and silence into meaning. The flowers stank; the two families — hers, my father's —

only served to make her death seem useless, impractical. It was not military — it did not have the startling energy and purpose of battle surrounding it — or the direction of political philosophy. Beside it, she and all of us who lived seemed hopelessly superficial.

"Well, Nickie, are you going to take good care of your father?" someone would ask. "You're all he's got."

I nodded, hearing that from almost all my aunts. Invariably strong, matronly embraces and long looks at my face, my uniform, my ribbons followed it. These were my parents' sisters (my father had nine of them; my mother, six), and although I gratefully accepted those embraces at first, the more they were given, the more I regarded them as pieces of theatre to keep me close to home. Family was all: I had sinned in leaving my mother to serve a larger power. My aunts flocked around my father's mother, who lived for years afterward and dominated her daughters and my father the way they dominated everyone else. By contrast, my mother's sisters, reflecting her position here, seemed retiring.

"What are you going to do now?" my Aunt Sarah asked.

"Are you going back to the Army?"

"Marines," I said.

She was my father's sister, a big woman, intelligent, good-natured, and, as the film of my parents' twenty-fifth anniversary can only hint at, loud. "Marines... Whatever." She kissed me, embraced me, made me feel her tears against my neck. "Are you going back to that horrible place?"

"I have to," I lied, although I really didn't. "It's my job."

She stepped back and looked in my eyes. "What about your father and brother? Someone has to look after them. You're the oldest."

I shrugged. "I haven't thought about it yet," I said. "Sal's alright. And with my father, there's always Cora to help."

"Still, you're the oldest. You have to do these things."

Aunt Sarah embraced me again — but very carefully,

insistently, I pulled away. Boots, helmet, and combat uniform were gone, but as they used to insist in Quantico, you
can take the Marine out of combat, but never the combat
out of a good Marine. I kissed her, coolly, properly, my
hands on her shoulders, keeping her huge body at arms'
length.

"If you ever need anything, Nickie, just remember your
Aunt Sarah. I'm your godmother after all."

Without an instant's hesitation, I dropped my hands,
placed my right foot behind my left, did an about face, and
walked onto the porch of the funeral home to smoke — yes,
Mayra — to smoke a joint.

8.

That day and the one following were a series of scenes
like that, and I have often tried to tell Mayra about them.
As the family filed past the coffin, looked at my mother,
kneeling to say brief prayers, I felt increasingly embarrassed and bitter. If this was the end, what had I flown ten
thousand miles to fight for? It's easy to say my attitude
was a result of my mother's passing, or the war: too much
blood and violence, too much death. But it was more than
that. The wake, its emotions, my angry, jealous thinking
about my comfortable brother and sister, both of whom
looked at me as if I didn't belong, worked to push me deeper into my own private gloom.

My father, on the other hand, felt better as the days went
by. Except for the quiet, mournful crying that he fell into
upon entering the funeral home each day, he stayed close to
his family and talked easily to his mother and others. He
even joked occasionally with some of the visitors, and by the
night before the interment he looked pretty much himself.
We came home late and talked in the kitchen with Sal before
going to bed. He poured a shot of rye whisky for each of the

three of us and heated a cup of milk on the stove for himself. We turned on the radio for some music. I remember the Beatles coming on, not the song but their singing, and then a long, slow ballad of protest by a woman whose voice called to mind brooks, tall grass, and naked feet running through both while promising commitment and lifelong love as soon as the fighting in that stranger's "far-off, broken" land began to stop.

The three of us sat at the table, overwhelmed by the dark passion of her voice, the words it gave feeling to, and I, thinking of the land surrounding our own wife and mother's grave, knew that for us, or one of us at least, the fighting would likely never stop.

It was a difficult four or five minutes. The white light from the overhead fixture threw everything into relief, and suddenly the prospect of new life for a bereft father and two sons seemed hopelessly impoverished. My father sipped at the milk and the rye, loosened his tie, and rolled up his sleeves. I looked at Sal and smiled as he swallowed his whisky, and he, shifting his gaze to the ceiling, merely shook his head and slumped, as if a weight had been loaded on, and then taken off, his shoulders.

"There's a lot of room in the house," my father said hopefully. "The three of us could be very comfortable. You boys are welcome as long as you like."

He squeezed Sal's shoulder and patted my arm, saying, "I mean it," and kissed my cheek. Seeing tears in both his and my brother's eyes, I flinched, not because of love, but because I felt confined.

After a few seconds I kissed him back and said, "Thanks, Pop. I'll probably finish my tour. I'm on short time now, and it's nice to know I can come back here."

Sal said nothing, but out of the corner of my eye I could see him watching me. My father nodded. We finished our drinks and bid each other goodnight. Sal went off to be with his girlfriend, telling me not to wait up for him, and so I sat up alone, as I often would in the next six months, smoking, rocking in a cane chair at least as old as I was, catching up to the latest music and listening to the noises of the house as I thought about Vietnam. My company came to mind, one or two real buddies who had been in country with me since the beginning. We had passed through some good times, and I thought of a few of them, some gross situations and jokes that were awful but had a veneer of hilarity about them because they took place over there.

I had been happier in the Marines than I ever was at home, and I knew it. Despite all my bitching, I could not deny the edge, the chill, even the fear in anticipation of putting everything, mind, soul, body, on the line for country and self. But what home was I fighting for if I did not wish to live there? What life, if it ended up in the ground, like my mother's? I had awful, awful thoughts, ones I could never tell anyone, least of all father and brother (or, later, wife and daughter). Suffice to say that the saner side of me wondered what I had been born to do if pointing a gun, pulling a trigger, and smashing a skull were the main pleasures and accomplishments of my life.

9.

I read quite a bit on the long flight home: letters, my mother's letters. We had not been close, mainly because I did not want to be, was not my mother's type of boy. Still, I received quite a few letters from her once I went away. During my fifteen months in country, she seemed to open up to me, tell me in letters things she had never revealed before: the difficulties she had loving my father, the temptations of men in her life, and, most revealing, an important affair, one with my favorite teacher, during which she actually stayed away from the house for several weeks, leaving my father and Cora to cope with Sal and me.

Perhaps it was the miles between us; perhaps she knew somehow her death was near. Or perhaps, as my wife Valerie once said to me, she simply never had anybody to write to before, making confession hard to resist. Whatever, she poured herself into those letters, telling me things I preferred not knowing, describing scenes from her youth and age I preferred not imagining, and yet as the MATS plane crossed the International Dateline that day after Tet, I felt grateful to her for the news. She had seen New York and Miami; she had crossed the ocean to Rome, stood praying in Vatican Square, handkerchief on her head, purse clutched in her hand, and stared at that balcony window for an hour to see the "chubby little Pope," as she called him, finally come to the railing and extend his hand.

All this while I thought she was in the hospital with, as the family called it, "woman troubles." My father, quiet, stoic, or perhaps simply ashamed, went through those days listlessly but methodically, rousing us from bed, feeding us, and driving us to school before going off to his own job. At night he and Cora cooked, and on weekends, both Saturday and Sunday, he took us to Aunt Sarah's for dinner. Sal, Cora, and I played with our cousins and when the adults' voices suddenly dropped as we entered their company, we assumed they were discussing my mother. But we thought, once again, her "woman troubles" occupied the conversation.

"I have lived so many lives," she wrote about a month before she died, "but nothing like the one I had during that week and a half in Rome with Aaron."

Aaron, or Mr. Zuder, as I knew him, was my fifth grade shop and crafts teacher, a man who loved wood, especially cherry and oak, and knew how to coax the most exquisite shapes and surfaces out of it, either by hand carving or lathe. A handsome, fleshy bachelor with a reputation for strictness among the students, he took my mother to Rome to visit the major sights but ended up preferring the small towns outside the city because their churches held more carved wood than marble. He had proposed to my mother in the sacristy of one of them, and even though she refused (he must have known she would: she couldn't leave her family for good, she told me), in the square afterward he bought her a foot-high statue of the Madonna and Child that had been carved from Italian chestnut. She had carried it in her bag when she returned to my father, but "out of respect" for him and her children, as she said to me, she left it in the attic, only to see it once or twice, usually around Christmas, in the following years.

There had been others, but Mr. Zuder was the one who stuck, she told me, always ready to welcome her into another life, "of travel, or passion," that she could never choose over her family. My father did nothing, suffering the sudden departures because, apparently, he had his own vices, though she never complained of them or told me what they were.

The one reminder of that adventure, she told me, was the print of the cherry trees that hung above our living room couch. After they returned, she had bought it for Mr. Zuder at a local art shop. But he had refused it, saying he couldn't take the print if she did not want to live with him. So she hung it in our house, our living room centerpiece, its pink, blossomy scene a comment on a part of life that she always wanted but couldn't keep.

10.

The morning of the funeral was sunny and hot. I felt relieved it was the last day I would have to wear my Class A's. When we entered the funeral home, my father and I kneeled before the coffin, and he, crossing himself after a moment, reached into it to pat my mother's hand. He had brought her diamond-studded wedding ring ("the dressy one," she called it) and asked the undertaker to put it on in place of the plain gold one she was wearing.

Unassuming and efficient as when we first met, my old school chum Digger Di nodded solemnly, but at the coffin he had difficulty. The old ring came off easily, but the diamond one, despite all his pushing and pulling, would not go on. My mother had always had trouble with that ring herself, which is why she only wore it on special occasions. Frequently, after a party or relatively formal dinner, she had to soak her hands in soap and water to free it. Sometimes it took several hours. So, we watched, horrified, as Digger, turning his back to us for cover, pushed and pulled at her ring finger. After a few minutes, he dropped his hands and asked the family to leave the room.

"Why?" I demanded, though everyone else seemed more than willing to cooperate. "Are you going to break her finger — or cut it off?"

"No! No, Nick, don't be silly. I would just feel more comfortable if the family weren't watching. For his sake." Digger nodded toward my father.

"It's okay, Nickie. Let him do it."

Shaking my head, and with visions of Vietnam atrocities, I left the room and waited with my father in the vestibule. Other members of the family arrived: Cora and her husband, Hank, a few aunts and uncles, all of whom shook our hands and said something about me or my uniform. We waited more than fifteen minutes with the door to the room closed. When Digger opened it finally, my father, Sal, and I took the three seats nearest the coffin. I saw the diamond ring on my mother's finger (the gold one had been slipped into my father's jacket pocket as we entered), but later I discovered that Digger had cut the ring open to make a proper fit. I was outraged, fuming, but as usual, my father was more reasonable: "It doesn't matter now," he told me. "As long as she has it with her."

I intended to complain to Digger anyway, but as I went

to find him my grandmother arrived on the arm of Uncle Ralph, and after helping him support her as she stood and prayed before the coffin, I forgot about the ring.

My grandmother made that happen. Prayer finished, she took the seat next to my father but held on to my hand. She studied me, her large, dark eyes virtually peering through me, trying to understand, I thought: the uniform, the ribbons, the absence of mourning black.

"*Come stai?*" she asked, not blinking behind her glasses. "You feel okay today?"

"*Sto bene, Nonna.*" I pulled my hand away. But she leaned toward me, and, thinking she wanted another kiss, I pecked her cheek.

"No, no," she said, pulling back. "One is enough. I want to look at you." She took hold of my sleeve. "You're a big boy now, a soldier. You have to take care of your father."

I nodded, my chest unconsciously expanding despite a wish to turn and run. After a long moment, she asked what I was planning to do.

"Do? When?"

"With your father, now that your mother has died."

I shook my head. "I haven't thought about it yet, Nonna."

She looked doubtful and squeezed my wrist, hard. Struggling for words in English, she said, "You and your father, you have each other now. You take care of him, but who is going to take care of you?"

"I'm a man now, Nonna. Don't worry. Besides, Sal and Cora will help." I kissed her cheek a second time and, embarrassed, started to move away. But she held my wrist, not letting me leave.

"Nickie, Nickie. What are we going to do with you?" She smiled, her eyes very deep and serious. Settling back in her chair, she looked at the coffin for a few seconds. "You don't know what it means to be without a mother, Nickie. You think hard what you want to do."

"I will, Nonna. Thanks."

I kissed her, or tried to, a third time. But she turned her cheek away, and my lips touched nothing but her hair. Blushing and laughing at myself, I stood up to greet some people just walking through the door.

The room was nearly filled now. In a few minutes Digger Di came in with Father Rossi and introduced him to me and the rest of the family. Correct but distant, I shook the priest's hand and tried to measure him for sincerity. There was very little to observe, I thought. He wore a dark suit and hat, which he took off and handed to Digger without looking. His thin, prominent nose gave him a suspicious, bird-like appearance while his voice, deep and confident, bespoke an acquaintance with enthralled, captive audiences. At the same time, both his bald head and wire-rimmed glasses threw off flashes of light, as if he were used to the dramatic pose at center stage. He leaned toward my father, talked with him and my grandmother a few minutes, to my mind avoiding the coffin. A hush had settled over the room since he entered, a respectful reaction to his collar that made me very, very uncomfortable. I still harbored illusions of making a funeral oration, I confess, but nobody had asked, and I lacked nerve or confidence enough to suggest it myself. Instead in a few minutes I watched enviously while Digger presented to the audience this stranger who, through confession, probably knew more about my mother's life than I did and, in addition, stood to receive from the family the attention I secretly coveted.

He drew a scarlet maniple from his jacket pocket and draped it over his collar. With a bowed head, he took a Bible out, opened it to a pre-selected passage and, the maniple flashing in the lights along with his glasses, raised his hand with a flourish. The hush in the room immediately deepened to absolute silence.

"Friends," he said. "And I call you friends, though I haven't met many of you before; it is sad to come together today, even though it is spring. This good woman has departed, leaving in grief husband, children and grandchildren, and all the rest who are friends and relatives. These are hard moments, particularly for you, Nicholas, and yes, you, my good lady, the mother of this now forsaken son. But remember that the good Lord always provides, and in this long moment of life, He is always prepared to help us in our solitude.

"Don't despair, I say. Don't lose hope, Nicholas. Despair is one of the deadliest of sins, and I say to you today that should you lose hope you will have given up your trust in Divinity. The deceased ... Sophie, led a rich, full life. And I assure you that although she is taken from us now, perhaps a little before her allotted time, she will live in the memory of her beloved husband, children, and the rest of us who gather here today. Life is indeed rich when we remember those who have gone before us. We may be grateful to God that He has created this woman, nourished her through years of youth and maturity, and now escorts her into the light of His angels' eyes. May we all live up to her performance, and may we all see her again when we too have passed beyond this valley to the other, kindlier one. Now, my friends, join me while I pray."

He turned, kneeling before the coffin, and I swear I saw him glance at his watch before re-opening his Bible. This was when I lost perspective. On my knees with the rest, I felt myself tremble with laughter, almost ready to call out something perverse. My mother looked pathetic in the coffin, surrounded by flowers though she was and paid respect by such a large assembly of people. It struck me as wrong that in a few minutes Digger would close the coffin lid, and we would never see her again, never make up for the wrongs that we, she, and the courses of our lives, had inflicted on each other. She had not been happy; her life had been more frustrating than meaningful, and I sincerely wondered how much I had contributed to her misery. Having lived a bare fifty-five years, she had just a few moments of laughter in a life that I saw as ending without regrets. There were moments when I thought of her in the ground, her flesh decaying slowly and painfully, and identifying her with that woman in Vietnam, I felt I might lose control. When I tried to block such thoughts from my mind, I looked at Father Rossi's darting head, heard what I imagined was a lack of commitment behind his words, and almost cried out until I looked at my mother and felt a real sense of relief. Her troubles were over.

Father Rossi stood after he finished, and people began to file past him to the coffin. My father left his seat first, but Digger officiously motioned him back to his chair and waved to those in the back of the room to come ahead. I heard a whine, quiet but gradually growing louder; when I looked around I saw my grandmother passing my father a handkerchief. He took it, weakly dabbing his eyes and nose, casting a miserable glance at my mother in the coffin. With her hand on his shoulder, my grandmother whispered in his ear. He nodded. "I'm sorry, Sophie," he said aloud. "I should have gone first. Don't leave me."

Sal and I took my grandmother by either arm and stood by her side as she said her final, inaudible good-bye. We escorted her to the vestibule then returned and stood together beside the coffin. "Good-bye," Sal muttered. Then, almost sportingly, "Good journey." I said nothing, mainly because my throat was full and I couldn't sort out my words. Sal looked at me. I looked at him and, after a moment, nodded. Without kissing her, we turned together toward my father and extended our hands.

He was silent, roughly pushing us aside as he walked to the coffin on his own. His eyes were clear, his head slightly cocked, and, as if he wanted to memorize something, he studied her with a quiet, I would have to say loving, adoration. He kneeled and stared as if he couldn't believe who she was. Sal and I stood behind but like Digger, who watched cautiously from the door, we were prepared to stop him from any rashness. I rested my hand on his shoulder, and after a few quiet seconds, he stood up. In tears, he leaned over to kiss her mouth. His voice became high, pleading. It was a sound I could not listen to.

"Oh, we'll miss you, Sophie. We'll be lost without you."

As he clung to her dress and pawed her diamond-studded ring, I gently, with Digger's nodding approval, pulled him away. He withdrew reluctantly, walking into the hall, but I turned back just before Digger closed the coffin.

"Wait a minute. I haven't done this yet." I bent over and kissed her on the cheek. Without warning, a sob burst from my throat and tears flooded my eyes. I squinted them back, clamped my mouth, and, after an angry glance at Digger, left the room.

The air was brisk outside. The sun shined pleasantly through the newly budding trees. Although I lacked a philosophic or religious focus on my mother's death, the fact that it was spring, that it was an incredibly warm and beautiful morning, provided a natural structure where — for the time at least — emotions took the place of words. The earth was soft, muddy, establishing a new growing year. From this perspective, the burial became a means of participating in life or, at least, touching a source of it. But of course, as a soldier I knew something about the false images nature could project.

"You know which car we sit in?" Sal said. He stood beside me on the sidewalk, nervously shifting his feet while staring past me to the street. Limousines lined the curb, with a flower car in the lead. The hearse, which we all kept waiting for, stayed in the driveway until Digger's pallbearers brought my mother to it.

"We take the front cars, don't we?" said my brother-in-law Hank, emerging from some people near the steps. "Those are for the immediate family, I think."

He grimaced and shuffled a little, his hands behind his back. We watched as more family cars pulled to the curb behind the limousines, and then at last the hearse left the driveway, stopping in front of the flower car while the pall-bearers carried the coffin to it. The moment was ominous. My mother always grew roses in our backyard, and she had sent several snapshots to me in Nam, of her among them on sunny afternoons. As a soldier, I had felt the photographs powerfully, especially after hearing that she was ill. As a mourning son I could not even think of them. In the photo-graphs she had worn her white hair cut short and set in a tight permanent wave. Her smile had struck me as relaxed and open, even though she and everyone else knew she was not well or happy. Still, with the roses, the smile, the hair shining in the sun, I had, in war, allowed myself to feel some hope.

Shortly Hank, Sal, and I went to the limousines, entering the first one with my father, Cora, and my grandmother. A gray limousine, with Digger, the priest, and the pallbearers in it, drove ahead of the hearse, leading us at a slow pace through the center of town, then out of it again until we reached the cemetery just beyond town limits. I watched my father as we rode, noting how calm he had become. He talked quietly in Italian with my grandmother, pointing to familiar landmarks and discussing them with her.

The gray limousine slowed at the entrance to the ceme-tery and waited while the rest of the procession caught up. Then gradually it led us along the winding roads until we came to a slope just before some railroad tracks. It was the last, most open part of the cemetery, with a view of grass, trees, and, in the distance, the main road that passed by. It seemed an appropriate spot for some reason. I have liked to think of my mother there because of the space and the sense of life and movement. Even the railroad track contributes something: In my imagination the whistle blowing at night reflects the energies and longings of my parents' lives.

My father started from the car immediately, but Digger trotted over and told us all to wait until the full line of cars had come to a stop. We watched the pallbearers, with Father Rossi following, bring the casket to the grave. Men with shovels stood near a pile of dirt, leaving when the pallbearers placed the casket on the ground. Then Digger nodded, and one of the drivers arrived to open car doors and tell us to get out. My father scrambled from his seat immediately, breaking into a trot across the grass. Sal and I helped my grandmother and followed.

Strangely, I kept waiting for something to happen, a special event — wonderful or awful — to mark the occasion. And, I confess, despite my uniform I was relieved to be unarmed, for inside, something was losing shape. When the priest raised the crucifix, I half expected the coffin lid to fly open and see my mother step out to announce her love for Mr. Zuder. Then, as Father Rossi started to pray, a V of geese flew over, honking, and I found myself nodding and laughing at them, as if I understood. I remembered groves of deep green foliage concealing dismembered bodies and thriving, blood-spattered plants with fingers, toes, or genitals beneath them; or cows, grazing and chewing contentedly as other animals, or humans, screamed and died. This was a mistake. A lie. We must not shovel an ounce of dirt on that coffin.

I looked at my father, his head bowed, sobbing into my grandmother's handkerchief, and out of reflex felt angry and muddled at the same time. I knew it was perfectly human not to be able to deal competently with death. With all my experience, I knew there was no real answer to it all, yet I couldn't understand why I was the only one who seemed to feel uncertain. I might have screamed if someone crossed me. And if someone gave me a reason, even a small one, funeral or not I would have gone at him or her with my bare hands.

Still, the others seemed accepting, the pattern of their eye movements betraying only slight ambivalence: Father Rossi to the casket, then back to Father Rossi again, interspersing that with occasional random glances at the sky.

It was an empty few minutes, worse than all the hours at the funeral parlor. I tried to master the time by thinking of pleasant, natural things, roses, pendulums, cycles, gyres, anything to counteract the one-way movement I had seen in my mother's life. But war memories interrupted and I could only understand every amazing thing that had happened in the last few years with an idea that seemed too banal and obvious: the ultimate victory of nature over everything, the triumph of grass, undergrowth, and trees.

"We shall *rise!*" Father Rossi shouted. "The Lord promises in His Book. We shall *rise!* — And his Son will take each of us by the hand. So have hope Nicholas and his children; hope that you will see this wife and mother again and join with her in God's eternal love."

In the context of such reflections, Father Rossi consigned my mother's body to the grave and with a flourish of the crucifix stepped back as Digger's aids lowered the casket into the ground. Digger passed out stems of carnations and motioned to my aunts to place them on the coffin as they filed past. I didn't want to see or hear the stones and dirt hit the wooden lid, and was relieved, after dropping my flower on the slowly gathering pile, when Digger motioned everyone toward the limousines. In the confusion that followed, some searched for their cars, some stopped to shake hands, others left to meet at our house for a post-funeral luncheon. As I walked toward our limousine, Digger called my name, "Nickie," and automatically I pointed to my father as the senior person.

"No, I want to speak to you, Nick." He shook his head.

When I motioned to my father again, Digger pointed at me. "This is for you. I have to show you something important."

"Digger," I said, clenching my fists, "I'm not ready —"

"Nick, please."

He raised his finger to his lips and took my arm to lead me back to the site of the grave. The men had raised a lean-to to cover the work of filling it in. Digger pulled aside a flap of the lean-to and stepped behind it, motioning me in after him. I heard the thud of gravel and stones on wood and, scared as well as impatient, looked away.

"Come here, Nick, I want to show you this."

"Digger, please..."

"Look — the vault," he said. I stepped inside the lean-to and nodded. The men stood there, shoveling, smoking, now and then bending and tossing aside the flowers. They were quiet and respectful enough, but I was afraid of bizarre jokes being told and didn't want to listen to their humor. I started to leave again, but Digger held me back.

"Wait. Look, Nick. Here. It's concrete."

He lifted a portion of the ground cloth and pointed beneath it to something in the shadows. "Come here. I want you to see, so there won't be any disagreement later on. I want your family to like our work." He took my hand, rubbing it against a concrete slab that protruded slightly from the ground. It was the vault. In the corner, beneath the edge of the ground cover, I also saw the brown mahogany stain of my mother's coffin. For the moment, it seemed alive.

"The vault's cement; complete, four sides and the bottom," Digger said.

I felt impatient and confused, scared to the point of immobility. When Digger tapped my arm and pointed to the vault again, I turned on him suddenly, my fists before me, and with my chest and legs pushed him against the lean-to pole. Holding my breath, I said, "Terrific, Digger. But what's it for?"

His glasses flashed in the light, and he spoke, gently, I must admit. "I'm sorry, Nickie, but someone should know these things. It's a wooden box, but no rain will get in. No water from underground. The, ah...; your, ah...; it will stay dry."

"The casket?" I said.

"The uh ..."

It dawned on me. With a note of stupid triumph I shouted, "Oh, no! No! Even Digger Di, the Friendly Undertaker, has his confusions!"

He shrugged, now looking impatient and confused himself. "It's in the contract, Nick. Some people question it when we send the bill. By then, of course, it's too late. Like Mr. Zuder used to tell us, you have to finish things right, completely, according to contract."

"Mr. Zuder said that?" I looked at him.

"You remember Mr. Zuder, the shop teacher: a perfectionist, a real stickler for details."

I said nothing. We started back to the cars together, smiling.

"I owe him a lot," Digger said.

At the road I shook his hand and Father Rossi's — telling the priest he'd delivered a well-constructed sermon. And although I wasn't ready to crack completely, I was close. I needed to hide, couldn't wait, in fact, to enter our limousine. Sal and Cora sat there. Hank, my father, and grandmother had switched to a family car to go directly to our house. As I got in, a jet flew overhead, breaking the sound barrier. Barely suppressing a shout — and giggle — after the sonic boom, I sat next to Cora and, wordless, held her arm.

She, Sal, and I looked at each other in silence as the driver started the engine and drove away.

ABOUT THE AUTHOR

FRED MISURELLA is a Fulbright scholar who has published fiction and nonfiction in *Partisan Review, Salmagundi, The Village Voice, The New York Times Book Review, VIA, Italian-Americana, The Christian Science Monitor, L'Atelier du Roman,* and other magazines and journals. He lives with his wife and son in Pennsylvania and teaches writing, journalism, and Italian-American literature at East Stroudsburg University. Email: fmisurella@po-box.esu.edu.

www.ingramcontent.com/pod-product-compliance
Lightning Source LLC
Chambersburg PA
CBHW022154260626
47155CB00018B/1928